Point of Snow Return

Alaska Cozy Mystery
Book 14

Wendy Meadows

Chapter One

Sarah nearly dived down onto the couch to rest in a warm living room. Feeling grateful to be home and far away from her insane cousin, who had nearly driven her bonkers, she placed her head into a brown couch pillow, closed her eyes, and sighed. "Conrad?" she mumbled, hungering to drop off into a deep sleep. "Remind me to never visit Michigan again."

"You can count on it." Conrad smiled as he sat down next to Sarah and began rubbing her back. Having Sarah back home in Alaska was a huge relief. Conrad hated when his wife wasn't within a twenty-minute drive from him. Who knew her trip to Michigan would have turned out to be fraught with murder? "When you're rested, I'll tell you about the call I had with Dr. Wester."

Sarah slowly raised her face up off the brown pillow and rolled over, careful not to get the blue dress she was wearing all tangled up. She looked up into Conrad's handsome face. Even though her mind was absolutely exhausted, Sarah was anxious to hear the news. "You sounded hopeful on the phone."

Conrad gently brushed Sarah's bangs away from her beautiful eyes with a tender hand. "Well," he began in a careful voice, "I'm not certain if I should be overly hopeful. You see, Sarah, Dr. Wester had suggested we try some type of new procedure that sounded extremely complicated and confusing to me. But," Conrad emphasized, "the success rate of this new procedure…which is still being run on a trial basis…is somewhat impressive…at least according to Dr. Wester."

Feeling her mind slowly crawl out of the sleepy hole she was trapped in and enter some sunlight, Sarah leaned up, threw her legs over the side of the couch, and focused more intently on the subject at hand. "What is this procedure?" she asked.

"Maybe it would be wise to call Dr. Wester tomorrow and have her explain," Conrad suggested. "I've never been good at…the girl stuff, you know? All I can say is that Dr. Wester believes you're a perfect candidate for the procedure and that our insurance would approve a trial run."

A mixed feeling of hope and dread entered Sarah's heart. She quickly stood up, walked over to a lovely fireplace holding a cozy, warm fire, and grew silent for a minute. What if Dr. Wester had finally discovered a cure for her inability to have children? What if the cure…failed? Sarah felt like she could burst into a million little pieces. "It seems like we've been trying forever," she whispered. "I want a baby…I'm so desperate to become a mother."

Mittens wandered into the living room, walked over to Sarah, and plopped down at her feet. Sarah smiled at the dog. "Mittens missed you," Conrad said.

"I missed her, too." Sarah bent down and began scratching Mittens's ears. "I see you've been taking care of my husband, girl. I'm very grateful." Mittens wagged her tail and let out a happy bark. Sarah smiled. "Have you been keeping my husband away from the carrot cake?"

Conrad slowly lifted his right hand and nervously scratched the back of his neck. "Well…as it turns out, Sarah…dear…honey…it seems that Mittens likes carrot cake, too."

"Oh, Conrad," Sarah said, "you know sweets aren't good for a dog."

Conrad winced. "Yeah…I know."

Sarah rolled her eyes. Men. "How much cake did you give Mittens?"

"Two slices…one slice this morning before you arrived home…total of three…dear…honey…"

Mittens let out another happy bark. Carrot cake was great. Sure, dog food wasn't exactly poison—and some dog food tasted pretty good (at least the wet kind—the dry kind was yucky). But carrot cake…oh boy! Carrot cake was grand! Only Sarah didn't seem to think so and Mittens wasn't sure why. What was wrong with carrot cake?

"Conrad, we have dog food for a reason," Sarah said, patting Mittens's head. She stood up. "No more sweets for Mittens, okay?"

"Yes, dear, of course," Conrad promised and gave Mittens a *sorry, girl* face. "The boss has spoken." Mittens threw two hairy paws over her nose and let out a sad whine.

Sarah rolled her eyes. "That doesn't cut the cheese," she told Mittens. She looked at Conrad and grinned. "You two are a pair. Someday if…when…we bring a child home…I have a feeling he or she won't be very bored with you two around."

Conrad rubbed the back of his neck again. "Sarah, speaking of having a child…well," he said, nervously looking down at the floor and then sighing. "What I mean to say is…what if…I do something wrong? I mean…what if I…don't learn how to warm a bottle properly…change a diaper…what if I drop the baby?"

"You won't drop our baby, sweetie," Sarah promised.

"It could happen," Conrad fretted. He quickly began pacing around the living room. "I've been doing a lot of thinking and I've come to the conclusion that maybe I shouldn't hold the baby until he…or she…is around ten years old, huh?"

"Oh, honey," Sarah giggled, "you're not going to drop our baby."

"What if I put a diaper on backward or…wipe toothpaste on a diaper rash instead of baby rash cream…or…just mess up the scene altogether?" Conrad asked as sweat began to slip down the side of his face. The poor man was scared stiff. "I know I've been acting calm and in control, Sarah, but the truth is…the idea of a baby scared me senseless. I mean, I've seen mothers out with their babies countless times when I lived in New York…in the parks, going to school…stores. But…those babies were seen from a distance. I could offer a polite smile at the kid and move on…but to be responsible…"

Sarah walked over to Conrad and took his left arm. "Honey, you're going to make a great dad," she promised. "I know it's natural to be a little nervous…but look at it this way…" Sarah paused and began searching for encouraging words as she studied Conrad's scared eyes. "If we mess up," she finally spoke, "our baby will not grow up to hate us."

"That's not very helpful."

"Oh, honey," Sarah insisted, "we're going to be great

parents." Sarah motioned around the living room. "We have a warm home…financial security…even a guard dog."

"I wouldn't call Ms. Chocolate Nose a guard dog," Conrad pointed out, sighing and kissing Sarah's nose. "I guess I'm a little scared. I've never been a dad before. Raising a baby is a huge deal."

Sarah placed her head against Conrad's chest and wrapped her arms around him. "I hope Dr. Wester is on to something," she told Conrad in a worried voice. "So far it seems like all we're doing is worrying over a baby that doesn't exist." Sarah closed her eyes. "But…you know what?" she said as the sweetest face Sarah had ever seen appeared before her.

"What?"

"I have a feeling…a…motherly feeling, somehow…that we're going to become parents, Conrad. I…have a feeling we're going to have a sweet, precious baby girl." Sarah focused on the gentle, soft face of a baby that was singing behind her eyelids. The baby was absolutely beautiful. "Someday soon…"

Conrad pulled Sarah closer. "Someday soon," he said just as Amanda knocked on the back door, let herself in, and found her way into the living room, drenched in snow. "Oh… did I interrupt something?" she asked, seeing Conrad holding Sarah in his arms.

"No…we were just talking about having a baby." Sarah smiled. She let go of Conrad, kissed his nose, and then walked over to the warm fireplace. "How is the coffee shop?"

"Everything is in order," Amanda stated in a tired voice. "The burst pipe is now fixed…if you can call a leaking pipe a burst pipe," she said and threw a hard eye at Conrad.

Conrad threw up his hands. "Hey, when Andrew checked

the shop, he said he saw water all over the kitchen floor. I assumed a pipe had burst from the cold."

"The pipe under the kitchen sink was leaking, Mr. Fix It," Amanda fired at Conrad. "Good grief, the blokes around this part of the world would think the sky is falling if it weren't for us women." Amanda joined Sarah at the fireplace. "Where's the little runt?" she asked.

"Manford flew to New York to see a friend," Conrad explained. "Or should I say an old girlfriend?"

"Oh?" Amanda asked and then grinned. "Why, that short little Romeo."

"That short little Romeo better remember his manners," Sarah warned.

"Relax," Conrad assured Sarah, "Manford isn't going to come back to Alaska with a wife. From what he told me, this girl he's going to see is…how can I put it?" Conrad thought for a second. "Manford said his heart still beats for a girl that would rather punch his lights out than kiss him…good enough?"

"Then why—" Sarah began to ask.

"Manford didn't say," Conrad confessed. "I didn't press him. You know how Manford is, honey. If you press him, he clams up. Besides, guys…understand each other."

Sarah began to worry about Manford. "What if he's in trouble?"

"Going to see a girl who is a cop…I don't think so."

"A cop?" Sarah asked Conrad. "Manford doesn't like cops. He can barely stand you."

Conrad shrugged. "A pretty girl in uniform is enough to make any man smile."

"Watch it," Sarah warned.

Conrad threw his hands up into the air. "Honey, you know what I mean," he pleaded. "Manford is a sap for pretty faces. Whoever this girl is…this cop…I'm sure she isn't a dog…no offense, Mittens." Mittens let out a low growl.

"I have to agree with that bloke," Amanda said, tossing a weary thumb at Conrad before continuing. "Manford is a little Romeo with the ladies."

Sarah wasn't so sure. She hurried to the coffee table, dug her cell phone out of a white purse, and called Manford. Manford picked up on the third ring. "Manford—"

"I'm at a birthday party," Manford yelled into his cell phone, surrounded by kids racing around a crowded backyard, screaming and hollering. "I can't talk now."

"A birthday party?"

Manford checked the silly clown costume he was wearing and then smiled at a pretty woman wearing a cop uniform. "Jessica…I owed an old friend a favor, okay?" Manford explained. "I'm pulling off a clown bit for her kid's birthday party. Besides, she wants me to be the best man at her cousin's wedding in a couple of days…no one else wants to."

Relief washed through Sarah. "Clown…birthday party… favor…wedding…got it, sweetie."

"Talk to you later," Manford yelled over the sound of screaming children. As soon as he ended the call, a ten-year-old boy with bright red hair kicked his leg. "Hey…what's the deal, kid!"

"Hey, stupid, you're supposed to be entertaining us and not talking on the phone!" the kid yelled, kicking Manford again and running off. Oh, the joy of being a clown.

Sarah put her cell phone away. "Manford is performing at a birthday party," she explained.

Amanda grinned. "So much for romance."

Sarah imagined Manford dressed as a clown, stuck at a birthday party, and trapped in the sounds of screaming children…and grinned. "Yeah, so much for romance," she said and then laughed. "Okay, who wants some coffee?"

"Me!" Amanda raised her arm up into the air and began shaking it. "Oh me, love…me, me, me."

Conrad glanced at the front living room. It was growing dark, and from the sounds of the winds, a storm was about to barrel down on the small town of Snow Falls. Storms were becoming a normal routine, but still, Conrad thought, each storm seemed to bring trouble—a dangerous, deadly trouble in the form of a hungry killer. "I can use some coffee," he said as a bad feeling entered his gut.

Sarah smiled. "I'll make a plate of sandwiches, too," she promised. "Suddenly I'm not that sleepy anymore. As a matter of fact…maybe we can play a board game?"

"Anything but Scrabble!" Amanda burst out. She yanked off her brown coat and slung it at Conrad. "Your husband cheats."

"I do not…you dry muffin," Conrad barked and slung Amanda's coat back at her. "You're the one who uses those very British words no one can understand."

"It's not my fault you have no brain, you bloke!" Amanda griped and then pointed down at her dark brown dress with white stripes. "We British are far more intelligent than you Americans…no offense, Los Angeles."

Sarah grinned. "No offense taken, June Bug," she laughed and hurried out of the living room before an all-out war broke out. "Those two," Sarah laughed, hearing Amanda fire at

Conrad again. She walked into a warm, brightly lit kitchen with Mittens tailing behind and began to make a fresh pot of coffee. "Those two are a pair," Sarah laughed as she dipped sweet coffee out of a white coffee canister. "Those two are—" The telephone hanging beside the refrigerator interrupted Sarah. She put down the wooden coffee scooper and answered the call. "Hello?"

"Yes, Sarah?" a voice asked.

"Yes, this is Sarah Garland…I mean Spencer."

"Sarah, my name is Lara Wilston," a woman with a pleasant-sounding voice spoke. "I'm one of the nurses who works in Dr. Wester's office." Not a person alive knew Lara Wilston's real name—at least not the name she had invented for herself.

"Oh…hello," Sarah said as her nerves tensed up. "Is everything…okay?"

"I'm calling because Dr. Wester wants to schedule a meeting with you as soon as possible," Lara explained, keeping her voice pleasant.

"Is this in regard to the new procedure my husband was telling me about?" Sarah asked.

"I'm not certain," Lara replied. "Dr. Wester asked me to schedule an appointment at your convenience. That's all the information I have."

Sarah nodded. She understood Lara's position. "I would like to speak with Dr. Wester as soon as possible," she confirmed and then paused. "It seems like a storm is approaching so I'm not sure how the roads will be tomorrow…and with today being Wednesday…perhaps on Monday, if there is an opening?"

"Let's see…" Lara pretended to check an appointment

book with her voice. "Yes…will Monday at two o'clock be okay?"

"That should be fine, thank you."

"Okay, Sarah, I'll let Dr. Wester know," Lara announced, forcing her voice to remain pleasant. "We will see you then. Have a good day."

"You too." Sarah hung up the phone, bit down on her lip, thought for a minute, and then went back to the coffee. "I hope the roads will be passable Monday."

Far away in Anchorage, Lara Wilston tossed down a gray cell phone, walked over to a window on deadly legs, pulled back a dark green drape, and peered down at a snowy hotel parking lot. "Yes, Sarah," she whispered, "it's time to play… very carefully. After all, you killed the Back Alley killer…you killed my daddy. Now it's time to make sure you suffer."

Chapter Two

On Thursday evening, the telephone in Sarah's kitchen cried out. Sarah lowered a hot cup of coffee, glanced at the phone, and then looked at Conrad and Amanda. Conrad was studying a very complicated Scrabble board, rubbing his sharp chin like a man trapped in a complicated riddle. Amanda, on the other hand, was grinning from ear to ear. She had managed to play a strange but accepted British slang word that Conrad argued was foul but the Scrabble dictionary gave a green light to. The word earned Amanda seventy-eight points, creating a comfortable lead over poor Conrad.

"I guess I should answer the call." Sarah sighed, put down her mystery novel, and hurried to answer the call. "Hello?"

"Yes, Sarah?" Lara asked.

Sarah recognized Lara's voice. "Yes?"

"I'm afraid I have some horrible news," Lara spoke, pretending to be close to tears as she calmly walked back and forth in front of the bed in her hotel room. The room was extremely fancy and modern, offering every comfort and luxury that money could buy. Lara Wilston was a very wealthy woman. At the age of twenty she had married a powerful, rich old man who was well into his seventies. Four years later, the old man finally started sleeping under six feet of dirt, leaving Lara with over twenty-two million dollars—money she was currently using to extract a hideous revenge on an unsuspecting woman.

"What's wrong?" Sarah asked, hearing the woman on the other end of the phone speaking in a broken voice. Conrad raised his head and studied Sarah's face.

"Dr. Wester…didn't arrive to work this morning…she was found…dead in her home…" Lara deliberately allowed her voice to break. "It seems like she…committed suicide."

Sarah felt shock attack her startled mind. There she was, standing in a warm kitchen drinking coffee and reading a mystery book while her husband and best friend played Scrabble…and Dr. Wester was dead. "But…I've met Dr. Wester on many occasions. She was a pleasant woman… happy. Married to her husband for thirty-one years…"

Amanda gave Conrad a concerned eye. Conrad nodded. "We're all in a state of shock," Lara informed Sarah. "I'm… calling to cancel all scheduled appointments."

"Yes, of course," Sarah replied, feeling disappointment enter her heart. Dr. Wester had spoken of attempting a new procedure. Now the procedure in question was put on hold, perhaps even permanently.

Lara cleared her throat. It was time to manipulate Sarah using clever mirrors. "Sarah, you will need to find a new doctor," she explained. "All patients are asked to come to the office first thing Monday morning and take charge of their medical file. Can you still make the trip?"

"Of course," Sarah assured Lara. Taking possession of her medical file was vital.

"Anytime will do," Lara continued and then added in a careful voice. "But…if you can't make the trip, I'm due to travel to Snow Falls on Tuesday of next week to visit my cousin. If you would like, I can bring your medical file with me if you sign and fax me a form authorizing me to do so. We have many patients who live outside of Anchorage that will be making the trip…" Lara let her voice break again. "Dr. Wester was so sweet…I'm sorry…it's been a very unreal day."

"I understand," Sarah assured Lara, having no idea what the woman she was talking to even looked like. She didn't remember ever seeing her at Dr. Wester's office. All Sarah had to go off of was a voice—a voice that sounded sweet and caring, not a voice that was deceptive and deadly, hungry for revenge. "I can make the drive to Anchorage," she continued. She tossed a worried eye at Conrad and then stood silent for a few seconds, listening to the storm outside howl and scream. "But," she added, "if you don't mind bringing my file with you to Snow Falls when you drive up…that would be helpful."

"I don't mind," Lara promised, pretending to fight back tears. "I'll fax you over the proper form. There's another patient who lives in Snow Falls who has already faxed me the form. I really don't mind helping."

"That's very kind of you," Sarah told Lara and began wondering who else in Snow Falls had been seeing Dr. Wester. Dr. Wester was a very…well, expensive specialist. "If there is anything I can do in the meantime—"

"What can anyone do in a situation like this?" Lara asked in a distraught voice.

"Yes, that's true," Sarah agreed. "I'm so sorry."

Lara drew in a deep breath. "I need your fax number, please."

"Of course." Sarah glanced at the back door, listened to the winds scratching and crying to get inside, and then gave Lara the fax number assigned to her cabin.

"I'll fax you over the form within the next hour, Sarah," Lara promised. "I…" She pretended to start crying. "I'm very emotional…please forgive me."

"It's understandable."

"I guess," Lara said. "I'll call you Tuesday, okay? Goodbye." Lara ended the call and grinned. "Oh yes, Sarah, I'll see you Tuesday," she promised. She walked over to a fancy wooden table sitting on a lush white carpet, sat down, and studied the delicious box of pizza. Sure, a woman pushing forty-three didn't need to eat a large pizza, but so what? Lara Wilston was a beautiful model who still made the younger girls back down in shame; or so she believed. In reality, Lara's beauty was quickly fading. The long, silky black hair that had been her trademark was slowly turning gray, each strand of gray stealing her youth. Lara refused to accept this fact. She refused to accept the fact that eating a large pizza and vomiting it back up was unhealthy, too. She was a woman trapped in the body of a forty-three-year-old woman but in the mind of a seventeen-year-old girl. Yet, even though her mind had never left the halls of high school, her daddy…the Back Alley killer…had taught her how to think like a killer. "Yes, Sarah, I'll see you…but not Tuesday. I want to play with your mind first." She laughed, snatched up a slice of cheese pizza, and began gobbling the food down like a hungry dog that hadn't eaten in weeks.

"Sarah?" Conrad asked, watching his wife slowly hang up the phone as if she were releasing a funeral cloth. *I'm back.* A hideous snowman wearing a leather jacket and chewing a candy cane grinned. *I'm back, Sarah…murder has returned…let it snow…let it snow…let it snow.* "Sarah?" Conrad asked again as Sarah's beautiful face twisted into a painful cry.

"Huh?" Sarah heard her voice float across the kitchen from a distant land as she stared into the eyes of the hideous, grinning snowman.

"The phone call?" Conrad asked. He calmly stood up, walked over to his wife, and studied her troubled eyes. "What's wrong?"

"Dr. Wester…she was found dead in her home earlier today," Sarah confessed, feeling her face turn pale. *You can never kill me, Sarah…the snow will always fall…the snow will always fall!* The hideous snowman hissed and then melted down into dirty snow lining the streets of some crime-riddled city. "That was Lara Wilston, one of the nurses that works in Dr. Wester's office," Sarah explained. "She needs me to pick up my medical record."

Conrad looked over his shoulder at Amanda. Amanda stood up, saying, "Sure, love, we can drive—"

"No," Sarah cut Amanda off, "Lara is faxing me over a form that will authorize her to bring my medical file to Snow Falls on Tuesday. Someone else in town is seeing…was seeing…Dr. Wester. Lara said she is going to be visiting her cousin here and doesn't mind bringing us our medical files. I have to sign the form and fax it back to her."

Conrad studied Sarah's words. He guessed what Sarah

announced sounded legal and logical. After all, in Alaska, folks traveled out of their way to see a good doctor if they didn't live in Anchorage or Fairbanks. A small town like Snow Falls was far enough away to wear down a car seat. It didn't seem strange that a nurse who was supposedly going to visit Snow Falls offered to do a good deed. But still…something in Sarah's words bothered Conrad. "I've never heard of that nurse, have you?" When Sarah shook her head, he said, "I want to confirm that Dr. Wester is…deceased, okay?"

Sarah looked into Conrad's eyes, read his concern, and nodded. "Call Andrew and confirm."

Amanda folded her arms and waited for Conrad to make the call. Ten minutes later, Conrad hung up the kitchen phone, walked over to the kitchen counter, and stood silent for a minute. "Dr. Wester is dead," he finally spoke. He leaned back against the kitchen counter, shoving his hands down into the pockets of the blue jeans he was wearing. "Authorities down in Anchorage are claiming possible suicide."

Sarah slowly placed her hands into the front pockets of the deep green dress she was wearing. The dress, usually very warm, suddenly felt cold. "I see," she said in a low voice as her mind struggled to seek practical explanations instead of running off a cliff like a madwoman who was quickly going insane.

Amanda brushed the back of the gray wool dress she had chosen for the day under her legs and sat back down at the kitchen table. "I'm not sure if we should be worried or not," she said. "I mean, love, the death of Dr. Wester did take place down in Anchorage."

"Yes, that's true." Sarah nodded. Her mind began to think about a pleasant woman in her early sixties who always had a sweet, caring smile on her face and warm eyes full of life and passion. Dr. Wester was not the type of woman who would end her life. Sarah was certain of that fact…or was she? Sometimes a suicidal person was the best actor in the world; a person could never really know. "Dr. Wester appeared to be a pleasant and caring woman…it seems strange that she would end her own life."

"Well," Conrad offered, "I've seen my share of people trying to lunge their bodies off a bridge. I've also seen my share of people wanting to end their lives but crying out for help instead." Conrad glanced down at the wooden kitchen floor, listened to the storm, and then shook his head. "What it comes down to is you never know what's going on inside a person's head. If a person wants to die…he or she will find a way to die. I mean, I've seen a heart doctor who helped save countless lives try to jump off a bridge…why?"

Sarah listened to Conrad with focused eyes. "Are you saying Dr. Wester's death isn't connected to us?" she asked.

Conrad shrugged. "I don't see how it can be. I know Dr. Wester was our doctor, Sarah," he explained, "but she also had a long list of other patients. Maybe the woman…just ended it, huh?"

"Maybe." Sarah sighed, feeling her mind step back onto the shores of logic and rational thinking. "We'll need to locate another specialist…in time."

"In time," Conrad promised. He looked at the kitchen table, saw the Scrabble game, and shrugged his shoulders again. "I guess we can call the game, Amanda, if you want."

"Under the circumstances," Amanda said, "I think your suggestion would be wise. And besides," she couldn't help adding. "I won." Conrad rolled his eyes.

Sarah walked over to the back door, checked the lock, and then listened to the storm scream and howl, scream and howl, like a madman hungry to devour her sanity. Dr. Wester was dead…and for a brief moment the snowman had returned…but did that mean anything? Sarah slowly touched her stomach and then closed her eyes. "Hold on, baby…mommy is still fighting," she whispered.

Conrad made his way over to Sarah, placed his hands down onto her tender shoulders, and studied the back door. "We'll locate a new doctor, Sarah," he promised. "Dr. Wester wasn't the only in the state. Besides," he added, "I was starting to think seeing a specialist out of state might be a better idea."

Sarah turned away from the back door. "Really?" she asked.

"I know this Jewish doctor in New York…man is a genius," Conrad explained. "I can give him a call and see if he will recommend someone if you want?"

"Perhaps…tomorrow?" Sarah offered. "I know this might sound strange, but I feel like we need to take tonight and remember Dr. Wester."

"That doesn't sound strange, love," Amanda promised. "I know I only met the woman one time, but you did tell me she was married, right?"

"For many years…she even had grandchildren," Sarah confirmed.

"Grandchildren…goodness," Amanda gasped. "It…it really doesn't make sense, does it? A successful doctor…a surviving marriage…grandchildren…it just doesn't make sense."

"The authorities are ruling Dr. Wester's death a suicide for the time being but that could change," Conrad told Amanda.

He bit down on his lip and then shook his head. "No," he said.

"No what?" Sarah asked.

"No to standing around," Conrad stated. He walked to the kitchen phone, snatched it up, and called Andrew. "Yeah, hey, can you make a call to that friend of yours in Anchorage and see if he can let me in on the Wester case? I want to confirm with my own mind that the woman ended her life or if she was murdered…Okay…I'll be waiting for your call." Conrad tossed the phone down and looked into Sarah's alert face. "It seems more practical…and safe…to have our eyes exploring every dark alley, Sarah."

"I'll pack our bags," Sarah confirmed.

"Hey, don't forget about me," Amanda exclaimed, pouncing to her feet. "I'm not being left alone."

"Then it looks like we're all three taking a drive down to Anchorage as soon as this storm lets up and the roads are passable," Conrad announced. He walked to the kitchen table, picked up a brown coffee cup, took a sip of coffee, and studied the Scrabble game. "If Dr. Wester was murdered, then we could be in for a different type of game."

"If?" Amanda repeated. "I hate the word 'if.'"

"So do I," Sarah agreed, turning her eyes back to the back door and thinking about Dr. Wester. Was the doctor's death somehow connected to her? And if so…why…how? Sarah touched her stomach again. Somewhere deep inside her heart —somewhere hidden and forbidden—she knew. "Hold on to mommy, sweet baby…someday you'll be in mommy's stomach…someday when the snowman is dead," Sarah whispered, feeling colder than she had ever felt in her entire life; a cold created by fear…a deep, vicious, cruel fear full of poisonous fangs anxious to devour a person's heart. "Hold onto mommy, baby. Please hold onto mommy."

Far away in Anchorage, Lara walked out of the brightly lit bathroom, made her way back to the wooden table, and picked up a photo of Sarah standing next to Conrad on a snowy sidewalk. "You will suffer," she hissed at the photo and threw it down. "You will suffer."

Chapter Three

"This storm might not ever pass," Conrad complained.

Andrew watched Conrad walk away from the window in his office on impatient legs. The detective appeared anxious to make tracks to Anchorage. "Nothing is moving out there," he told Conrad. "If you have a pair of skis or a snowmobile, you might make it a few miles before turning into a penguin."

"It's Tuesday," Conrad continued to complain. "Sarah and I were supposed to be in Anchorage today."

"I know," Andrew told Conrad, leaning back against the office door and scratching at his uniform. Old Lady Mayes used far too much starch once again. Andrew felt like he was trapped in a giant pool of poison ivy. Starch made him itch like crazy. But, he tried to console himself, at least his uniform was in tip-top shape (like it mattered; no one was occupying the police station except Andrew and Conrad). "We can't control the weather, Conrad. You might as well accept the fact that this storm is going to continue squeezing this town for another day or two."

"The storm seemed to be letting up Saturday night." Conrad plopped down behind his desk. "And then Monday… boom! The storm returns with a very bad attitude."

"That's the way of Alaska," Andrew said, feeling his mind return to a hunting trip he had taken with his dad at the age of sixteen. He saw a large man and a skinny kid hunched down in a pathetic little cabin trying to stay warm beside a miserable fire. "Conrad, I remember when my old man and me got trapped in a storm that would make this one seem like a dream," he said. "We were hunting up farther north when this storm came barreling down at us like a freight train thundering down on a stalled car. My old man and me, man, we barely made it back to the hunting cabin we were staying in."

"What happened?" Conrad picked up his coffee cup, checked the contents, and shook his head. "Obviously you lived through the storm…so what's your point?"

"My point is my old man and me nearly died," Andrew told Conrad in a serious voice. "The storm produced wind gusts so strong that half of the room in the cabin was ripped clean off." Andrew held up four fingers. "For four days my old man and me were forced to hunker down in that cabin and grit our teeth…freezing our back sides off…eating nothing but beef jerky…eating snow for water…peeing in a corner." Andrew shook his head. "Those four days taught me to respect the weather, Conrad. I know you're upset and all, but you're just going to have to sit tight and wait for this storm to pass."

Conrad checked the inside of his coffee cup again. "You

heard what Detective Eastbrook said, Andrew. The man no longer thinks Dr. Wester ended her own life."

"Yeah, I spoke to Matthew," Andrew replied in a worried voice. "He told me that the drug found in Dr. Wester's system killed her before she drowned."

"There was enough OxyContin in Dr. Wester's system to kill a herd of elephants," Conrad pointed out, tossing down the empty coffee cup in his hand. He snatched up a piece of paper. "This is Dr. Wester's autopsy report," he continued in a troubled voice. "I…don't know if I should show it to Sarah or not." Conrad eyed the report with troubled eyes. "I'm not sure if Dr. Wester's death is connected to Sarah or not, Andrew, and I have no idea why it would be, but my gut is throwing up a whole lot of red flags."

"I read the report," Andrew told Conrad, walking over to the office window and peering out into the vicious storm. "Matthew told me she didn't have an enemy in the world… had a great marriage…great job…great life."

"Maybe a patient or a staff member got at Dr. Wester?" Conrad suggested as his eyes examined every word on the autopsy report. "A woman who might blame Dr. Wester for being unable to get pregnant…a staff member that was fired? Who knows?"

"Matthew is running every patient and staff member," Andrew assured Conrad as he studied the storm.

"If it's okay, I would like a list of every patient and staff member," Conrad requested. "And speaking of staff members, a woman named Lara Wilston was supposed to bring Sarah her medical file today. Sarah called this Lara woman and canceled since we decided to drive to Anchorage." Conrad placed the autopsy report down, picked up a pen, and began tapping his desk. "This Lara said another woman in Snow Falls was seeing Dr. Wester…guess that could be true."

"But?" Andrew asked, finally turning away from the window.

"Andrew, one visit to Dr. Wester's office…just for a consultation…costs enough to drain a year's salary," Conrad explained. "We're talking about some serious money."

"And you're implying that the people of Snow Falls are too poor—"

"I'm implying that Dr. Wester is a specialist that treats women having difficulty becoming pregnant," Conrad cut Andrew off. "Now, I don't know every single woman in Snow Falls, Andrew, but you do. Do you know of a single woman who might need to be seeing a specialist like Dr. Wester?"

Andrew rubbed his chin and thought. "My wife would know more than me."

"Then call your wife…please," Conrad pressed. He picked up the phone on his desk and held it out to Andrew. Andrew shrugged, took the phone, and called his wife. Conrad waited as the storm howled and hissed outside of his office window, digging at the glass with icy fingers. "Well?" he asked as soon as Andrew ended the call.

Andrew handed the phone back to Conrad. "My wife knows every single woman in Snow Falls," he said in a deep, thoughtful voice, rubbing his chin again. "Eight women living in Snow Falls are happily pregnant…and outside of those women, my wife isn't aware of anyone who is trying to become pregnant or is in need of a specialist."

"Call Detective Eastbrook and have him run Lara Wilston ASAP," Conrad ordered.

"I'm on it." Andrew snatched the phone out of Conrad's

hand and called Detective Matthew Eastbrook. "Yeah, Matt… it's Andrew…look, don't ask questions, okay…I need you to run a woman working for Dr. Wester named Lara Wilston… What?…You have the employee list on your person…great…"

A grizzly-looking man with a neatly trimmed black beard leaned forward in his brown leather chair and examined his extremely organized desktop. Matthew Eastbrook wasn't one for tolerating a messy desk, attitude, or life. At fifty years old, he prided himself on logic, intelligence, practicality, and common sense. Solid police work required a sound mind. Catching criminals required skill and experience—not the junk thrown onto TV screens that portrayed cops as heroes after one day on the job. "Let's see…Lara Wilston," he said, picking up a piece of paper that had been faxed to his office by a real nurse who worked in Dr. Wester's office. "Lara Wilston…" Matthew scanned the list all the way down to the bottom. "No, Andrew, there is no Lara Wilston on the list."

"There is no Lara Wilston working for Dr. Wester," Andrew confirmed to Conrad.

Conrad hit his desk with a hard fist. "Tell Detective Eastbrook that a woman named Lara Wilston contacted my wife."

Andrew relayed the message to Matthew. "I heard Detective Spencer loud and clear," Matthew informed Andrew and rubbed his phone ear. "I'll start an immediate search for Lara Wilston. However," Matthew advised, "at this point I wouldn't get my hopes up. But there are things you can do on your end to help—"

"Contact the phone company and track down the number that called Sarah's cabin. Yeah, I got it," Andrew assured Matthew and then tossed a worried look at Conrad. Maybe

Lara Wilston was in Snow Falls instead of Anchorage when she called Sarah to tell her about Dr. Wester's death? Could that be? Andrew didn't think so. The timing of the doctor's death wouldn't allow a killer the advantage to travel to Snow Falls between the time Dr. Wester was found and the time Lara Wilston contacted Sarah; unless Lara Wilston had a partner or hired a professional killer to murder Dr. Wester. Besides, the majority of the roads north of Anchorage were closed due to heavy snows. The state was working to clear the roads but was being hammered down by tough storms. "When you live in Snow Falls, you're on your own," Andrew whispered.

"That's the way of it," Matthew confirmed. "Andrew, Alaska may be considered a 'state' in the official sense, but in all truth the land is still wild, untamed, and raw. Where you live, my friend…well, you might as well be living on the moon."

"That's the way I prefer it…sometimes," Andrew replied, feeling pinned down by the storm. As much as the snow was home to him, the snow also hindered his ability to be a cop; not that Andrew was some great cop or a hero—he was only a normal man attempting to serve the community he loved.

Conrad reached for the phone. "Let me speak to Detective Eastbrook."

"Sure thing." Andrew handed Conrad the phone and waited.

"Detective Eastbrook—"

"Hello, Detective Spencer," Matthew said in a pleasant but professional voice. "Before you start chewing my ear off, rest assured I will do everything within my official capacity…and then a little more…to locate this Lara Wilston person. But you know as well as I do we could be searching for a shadow who gave—"

"A false name, yeah, I know," Conrad told Matthew, who shot to his feet and threw his eyes at the office window. "Lara Wilston offered to bring my wife her medical file from Dr. Wester's office," he continued. "This woman knows where my wife lives…knows her name…even killed Dr. Wester—"

"We're not sure of that."

"You will be," Conrad promised. "Now please, listen to me…I have a favor."

"Shoot."

"The building Dr. Wester's office is located in was soaked with security cameras. I counted ten cameras alone in Dr. Wester's office." Conrad paused, closed his eyes, and ran his mind back to a private office that smelled of sadness and hope at war with one another. The office, dripping with money, was fancy, resembling a museum more than a doctor's office. But what Conrad focused on the most was the door leading into the office. The door could not be opened unless the front desk person pressed a button that popped the lock. But before that event could take place, the visitor had to speak through an intercom and confirm to the receptionist that she had an actual appointment by stating her name and birthday. Conrad appreciated the security measures installed to protect women seeking hope. He'd never considered they might be used to help solve a murder. "I want you to—"

"Review the cameras?" Matthew asked. "I have a team already undertaking that tedious task, Detective Spencer. I know you are a cop from the tough streets of New York, but you're going to have to trust that cops in Alaska know their stuff, too."

Conrad slowly opened his eyes. "I'm sorry. It's just that my wife is in danger—"

"And as I recall your wife is one of the finest detectives to grace Alaska," Matthew pointed out. "Your wife, Detective Spencer, caught the Back Alley Killer and then managed to kill him when the snake showed up in Snow Falls."

"Well, it was Amanda who actually put a bullet through him," Conrad corrected Matthew. He let out a worried breath and then sat back down. "Hey, again, I'm sorry…worried husband, you know."

Matthew leaned back in his office chair. "Detective Spencer, I've known Andrew for a good many years and come to trust him as if he were my own brother." Matthew eyed a half-smoked cigar but decided against it. "Andrew has nothing but the highest respect for you, and that's good enough for me."

Conrad tossed a grateful eye at Andrew. "Andrew is a good man."

"And so are you," Matthew promised. "Don't worry, Detective, I'll work my end. If I come up with a grain of dust that might be important, I'll call you."

"I want to make tracks for Anchorage as soon as the storm that's holding Snow Falls captive lets up," Conrad told Matthew. "You gave me the green light to—"

"And the offer is still open," Matthew assured Conrad in an easy voice. "Detective, I've been married to the same lovely woman for thirty years now. I'm no stranger to being a husband. I understand the worries."

"Yeah…I guess you do," Conrad nodded. "Thanks, Detective—thanks, Matthew."

"Any time, Conrad." Matthew ended the call, studied his

organized desk, and then went to work. "Okay, Lara Wilston, let's see if you can be found or if the name you gave is a shadow name."

Conrad tossed down the phone, looked up at Andrew, and then pointed at the autopsy report. "Sarah and Amanda are down at the coffee shop with Mittens. I guess…I guess I better go have a talk with my wife, huh?"

"Conrad," Andrew stated in a careful voice, "Sarah may be your wife, but don't forget that she's also a cop—a brilliant cop. She's the type of woman who can take a punch and keep on making it to the next round."

"Andrew, Dr. Wester made it clear that stress is Sarah's enemy," Conrad replied in a voice that was about ready to throw in the towel. "I know my wife can run rings around the both of us when it comes to cop work…the woman beats me at chess in less than thirty seconds. But—"

"Sarah is also your wife and you guys are trying to have a baby. I understand," Andrew assured Conrad. "I remember when my wife and I first became pregnant…my nerves never settled until the doctor slapped my kid's butt and he let out a mighty cry." Andrew walked over to Conrad and squeezed his friend's shoulder. "You and Sarah are not alone, okay? We're family now."

A strange sense of comfort washed through Conrad. Yes, Andrew was…family. A lot of people in Snow Falls had become family; a family Conrad hadn't expected to make. "How can I tell Sarah?" Conrad asked in a pleading voice, turning Andrew into a brother rather than a friend. "Andrew, if Sarah finds out the truth…the stress…we'll never have a baby."

"I think Sarah already knows the truth," Andrew replied.

"Conrad, your wife isn't blind, and I doubt she's in town today because she decided it was a good time to spring clean the coffee shop."

"That's what I was afraid of." Conrad sighed, stuffed the autopsy report into his jacket pocket, and walked out of his office like a man walking toward a frozen teardrop that was slowly beginning to melt.

Chapter Four

Sarah handed Conrad a hot cup of coffee and waited for her husband to defrost before speaking. Judging from Conrad's face, the poor guy had ventured out into the storm with bad news swelling up like a wave inside of his heart. As a cop herself, Sarah understood the rules of the game, and one of the rules she stood by was to never press information out of someone who was being torn apart inside. Patience was not only a silent form of intelligence, but also a silent kindness. "The storm seems to be growing stronger," she said to Amanda rather than Conrad, as she walked over to the heavy wooden front door and listened to the storm. "I'm glad I wore extra layers under my dress today."

Amanda tossed a slow eye at the outfit Sarah had chosen to wear—the dress was a train wreck: a green, white, and red floral pattern. Uh, no. Sarah's beautiful complexion demanded plain, soft-colored patterns, not loud, dysfunctional…train wrecks. "Love, that dress…goodness."

"This dress is a gift from Manford," Sarah explained, pressing her back against the front door. She calmly watched

Conrad sip at his coffee and then walked her eyes around the front room. "Still feels like the 1940s in here."

Conrad knew Sarah was allowing him to settle his thoughts. He plopped down at a cozy wooden table, put down his coffee, and began rubbing his gloved hands together as snow began to melt in his hair and on his thick black winter coat. "Sarah…" he finally spoke, "there's been a change in the case."

"I assumed," Sarah told her husband. "I can read your eyes better than I can read my own eyes, honey."

"Yeah…I guess you can," Conrad agreed. He looked at Sarah, saw his wife perched at the front door as if she were a stone statue, and felt his heart break. Everything inside of the man wanted to protect Sarah from harm—but deep down inside, Conrad knew Sarah was a cop who could handle the rough cases. "Detective Eastbrook doesn't believe—"

"…Dr. Wester committed suicide?" Sarah asked. "I assumed."

"Why?" Conrad asked, hungry to know what thoughts were roaming around in his wife's head.

"I called Pete and had him do some checking," Sarah explained without moving away from the front door. She tossed an eye at Amanda, saw her friend standing beside the front counter wearing a dress that wasn't…such a train wreck—a plain but pretty gray and white dress—and continued. "I wanted Pete to check out all the employees working for Dr. Wester. I assumed Detective Eastbrook was running the employees and the patients, but my focus was more on the employees."

"Lara Wilston?" Conrad asked.

Sarah nodded. "Conrad, I can't recall meeting a Lara

Wilston at Dr. Wester's office. So I made a call to the office and spoke with Nurse Potter…you remember her, right?"

"About sixty…kinda plump…deep gray hair…tons of bad jokes?" Conrad asked.

Sarah nodded. "Nurse Potter determined for me that no woman by the name of Lara Wilston works or has ever worked in Dr. Wester's office."

"Why didn't you tell me?"

"I made the call early this morning," Sarah explained in a torn voice. "I couldn't bring myself to…walk into this dark alley until this morning. Why?" Sarah touched her stomach with a loving hand. "Maybe because I'm afraid…"

Conrad stood up and rushed over to Sarah. "Honey—"

Sarah looked into her husband's loving but scared eyes. "I struggled to be a cop in Michigan, Conrad…I didn't want to be a cop. The old man in Oregon…he helped me." Conrad felt confusion grab his mind. Sarah sighed. "In my heart the old man helped me," she explained. "I…I didn't want to fight the darkness anymore…there wasn't really a choice. I was hoping there was a choice this time."

"But there isn't, right?" Conrad asked as if someone was taking a knife and stabbing him.

"The more my mind began to chew on the name Lara Wilston, the more I tried to place the woman, something uneasy began to grow inside of my gut," Sarah confirmed. "Lara Wilston said a second woman living in Snow Falls had been a patient of Dr. Wester's…but who? Dr. Wester is a specialist…very costly. I'm not implying that a resident of Snow Falls wasn't seeing Dr. Wester, but…"

"Andrew called his wife," Conrad cut in and shook his

head. "Andrew's wife can't think of a single woman who might have been seeing Dr. Wester."

"Me neither," Amanda jumped into the conversation.

"Nurse Potter confirmed that no one by the name of Lara Wilston has ever worked in Dr. Wester's office...or the entire medical building for that matter. Pete backed up Nurse Potter's statement," Sarah explained, speaking in a straight voice. "If there is no Lara Wilston—"

"Then the woman who called you could have possibly lied about the second woman...and you're wondering why," Conrad stated.

Sarah nodded. "Yes," she confessed, struggling to make sense of the situation. "Conrad, whoever this woman is, she would have known the truth would be discovered sooner or later." Sarah slowly reached down into the pocket of her dress and pulled out the medical authorization form Lara had faxed her. "This form is legitimate, Conrad. I scanned it to Pete and Nurse Potter. Both confirmed that this is a legitimate medical authorization form. Whoever the woman I spoke to is...she seems to have a premeditated plan."

"Yeah," Conrad said in a deep, worried voice as his eyes studied the form Sarah was holding. "I guess I better show you this." Conrad reached into his coat pocket and pulled out Dr. Wester's autopsy report. "Seems like a high dose of OxyContin killed Dr. Wester before she drowned."

Sarah put the medical authorization form back into her dress pocket, carefully retrieved the autopsy report from Conrad, and began reading. Conrad walked back to the table he had sat down at, picked up his coffee, and waited for Sarah to examine the report. "Are there any cinnamon rolls?" he asked Amanda. "I'm a little hungry."

"Los Angeles and I were about to bake a batch before you arrived," Amanda said. "I have some bread and deli meat. Want a sandwich?"

"Please…but no mayonnaise…just plain meat and cheese."

Amanda rolled her eyes at Conrad. "I know you, silly bloke…you eat all of your meals plain. You and my hubby… plain blokes." Amanda threw her hands up into the air and roamed away mumbling to herself. "Plain meat and cheese… not even a hint of oregano…silly blokes…"

Sarah glanced over the autopsy report and watched Amanda vanish into the kitchen. "What would I do without that woman?" she asked Conrad.

"Have peace of mind?" Conrad offered.

"I heard that, you empty-headed bloke!" Amanda yelled from the kitchen.

Sarah sighed. "You two," she said and threw her eyes back down to the autopsy report. "It does seem that Dr. Wester died of a high overdose before she drowned," she confirmed. "The coroner found the injection site on the right side of Dr. Wester's neck…"

"Attacked from behind is my way of seeing it."

"Me, too," Sarah agreed.

"The location of the needle mark is what made Detective Eastbrook reconsider his position on suicide," Conrad explained. "One little needle mark…one little needle mark…" Conrad took a sip of coffee. "Whoever killed Dr. Wester could have easily made it appear as if the woman had injected herself, Sarah."

"I know." Sarah walked over to Conrad and handed him back the autopsy report. "The killer is playing a game…leaving breadcrumbs for me to discover. The question is…why?" Sarah sat down across from her husband, reached for his coffee, and took a sip. "I made a lot of enemies living in Los Angeles and you made a lot of enemies living in New York. If we tried to create a list of suspects—"

"We'd only be chasing our tails," Conrad told Sarah in a tired voice, feeling anger and desperation grip his heart. "We may not have the time to chase our tails."

Sarah took another sip of coffee. The brew was strong but good; a coffee that dared to stand up to the storm blaring outside the coffee shop. "It may be safe to say the killer is a female…but then the killer may also have an accomplice…or multiple accomplices?"

"What is your gut telling you?" Conrad asked Sarah, reading her intelligent eyes.

"My gut is telling me we're looking at one single person, Conrad," Sarah explained, put down the coffee cup, and focused on the front door. "Why do I think that?"

"I'm all ears, honey."

Sarah placed her hands together and sat silent for a moment, allowing her mind to wander out into the storm and search for the hideous snowman. "The snowman likes to work alone," she whispered. "Sometimes there may be more than one character in the murder…but there is only one killer the snowman forms a close friendship with."

A cold chill ran down Conrad's spine. "Sarah—"

Sarah kept her eyes out in the storm. The snowman was hiding…lurking in the icy white nightmare encompassing Snow Falls…waiting…waiting to attack. "He's out there… waiting."

Conrad lifted his hands and rubbed his chin. "Okay,

honey, let's assume that we're looking at one killer. We also have to assume that killer will eventually make her way to Snow Falls."

"I know." Sarah studied the storm one last time with dreadful eyes and then walked her thoughts back inside the warm, safe coffee shop. "Eventually…but not now. This storm will keep our killer at bay."

"How do we know our killer isn't already in Snow Falls?" Conrad asked.

"A gut feeling," Sarah whispered. "The snowman will come around more often when the killer arrives in town." Realizing that she was speaking like a woman who had gone insane, Sarah shook her head, focused her mind, and locked her eyes on Conrad. "Honey, what I mean is—"

"Sarah, I sleep right next to you at night. I watch you dream…hear your nightmares. I understand," Conrad promised his troubled wife. "You don't need to explain anything to me."

Sarah melted into Conrad's eyes and cuddled her frightened mind up against the man's heart. "When I first created the snowman, it seemed…innocent. The snowman was simply a fictional character in a book…something a killer left as a message to frighten his victims." Sarah looked down at her tender hands that were shaking a little. "When I relocated to Snow Falls from Los Angeles, I brought the snowman with me…after all, I am a writer, right? Sure. I simply couldn't leave all of the characters I created in Los Angeles. I had deadlines to meet…books to write…a new life to begin." Sarah paused as her mind returned to a warm, sunlit beach sitting outside of Los Angeles. The beach was deserted—staring out at a calm ocean that was tossing gentle waves down onto the shore.

Then, out of nowhere, loud thunder shattered the blue sky. Sarah threw her head up and saw a hideous snowman pulling the sky apart with black, ugly claws dripping with gray slush. *I'm here, Sarah…I'm here,* the snowman hissed as his eyes pulsated with red venom. Sarah heard herself cry out in fear and try to run away from the beach. The snowman let out a creepy giggle. Icy, rotted winds and poison snow began flooding from its mouth. The winds and snow caught Sarah and quickly formed a thick, sticky spiderweb. *You can never escape me, Sarah…never!*

"Sarah?"

Sarah didn't hear her husband's voice. Instead, inside of her terrified heart, she saw herself struggling to break free of the spiderweb…kicking and screaming…kicking and screaming. "Why did I ever create you!" she cried. "Why won't you go away!" *Because, Sarah,* the snowman hissed, lowering its body down from a grumbling black sky like a spider lowering its body down from a hungry web, *I'm murder…I'm what you decided to become.* "No!" Sarah screamed. "I became a cop to destroy you!" *No!* the snowman growled, placing its snarling face in front of Sarah. *You can never destroy me…instead you had to become me in order to stay alive…to survive the madness…the darkness…the pain.* "Leave me alone!" Sarah cried. "I brought you to Alaska with me…I let you live." The snowman grinned. *And that was your worst mistake.*

"Sarah?" Conrad spoke in a louder voice, watching his wife sit as if she were trapped in a trance. "Sarah?"

"Huh?" Sarah heard her voice slip through a crack in her nightmare and return back to the coffee shop.

"Are you okay, honey?" Conrad asked.

The snowman hissed at Conrad, climbed back up into the

black sky, flared down at Sarah with its red, pulsating venomous eyes, and then crawled away, taking the poison winds and snow with it. Seconds later, a bright blue sky appeared along with a soothing warmth. The warm air attacked the spiderweb holding Sarah hostage and destroyed it. Feeling her body receiving freedom, Sarah ran to Conrad's heart and wrapped her arms around it. "I'm...bad memory," she said in a shaky voice.

"I'm sorry."

"So am I," Sarah said in a voice that was still struggling to slap the last of the snowman's spiderweb off her. "I never knew becoming a homicide detective...facing murder...would do this to me, Conrad...would create a monster...a monster I actually started to depend on in order to survive...all the insanity."

"Murder is ugly and cruel," Conrad replied as the winds howled and screamed, clawing at the coffee shop and hungering to get inside and destroy everything that was good and noble. "We see the worst people can do to each other...we see an evil that attaches itself to our lives day after day, Sarah. Crime scenes...morgues...violence...you name it..." Conrad stopped talking. His words were certainly not helping Sarah. "Look, honey, we're going to find out who killed Dr. Wester... find this Lara Wilston person...and end this once and for all."

"Conrad," Sarah stated in a low, worried whisper, "all we can do is wait until the killer comes to Snow Falls. Just...wait." Sarah looked out the front door at the vicious storm that was taking the town of Snow Falls hostage, growing stronger by the minute. At that moment, what Sarah—or any citizen living in Snow Falls, for that matter—didn't know was that the storm was going to become one of the worst storms Alaska had experienced in over two hundred years. By the time the storm passed, Sarah would be changed forever.

"Here's your sandwich, you bloke," Amanda announced as she burst out of the kitchen. "I made us all a…" Amanda stopped talking when she saw Sarah's eyes. "Uh-oh," she said in a dreadful voice, "I know that look…and it isn't good."

Chapter Five

Night fell. The storm continued to rage. Sarah and Amanda huddled down in the coffee shop with Mittens, drinking coffee and eating turkey sandwiches. What else was there to do? It wasn't as if Sarah could throw on her coat and start patrolling every square inch of Snow Falls, kicking in doors, searching for Lara Wilston in homes filled with sleepy-eyed citizens battling the snow. No, Sarah was trapped inside her coffee shop. Not that being trapped inside of a building she considered her second home was a horrible punishment. The coffee shop was warm and safe and the generator—oh, the sweet generator—was working grandly, bravely taking over for the power that had been silenced about half an hour before night arrived. "Well, the phones are still up," Sarah informed Amanda in a relieved voice.

Amanda took a sip of coffee and watched her best friend study an old-fashioned brown phone that was sitting on the front counter. "What did Conrad say?" she asked.

"Detective Eastbrook is coming up empty-handed," Sarah

explained in a surprisingly calm voice. As a cop Sarah knew that police work took time—she also knew that a cop didn't always throw a handful of gold into an evidence bag. Police work was filled with deep bags filled with chance more than certainty. Crime didn't occur on a structured schedule and the criminal mind didn't operate under the guidelines of delusional psychiatrists who assumed they had the human mind all figured out; Sarah had yet to meet a psychiatrist who was mentally sound themselves. "All we can do is wait."

"Wait in this storm," Amanda told Sarah, walking her eyes around the coffee shop and letting out a tired smile. "You know, Los Angeles, other than waiting for a killer to show her face, tonight isn't so bad."

"Oh?" Sarah said.

Amanda patted the table she was sitting at. "Sit and let your dear old friend explain her thoughts, love." Sarah picked up a cup of coffee, walked over to the table, and sat down. Amanda picked up a half-eaten turkey sandwich that was resting on a green plate, took a bite, and continued. "While you were talking to Conrad, my mind wandered over to O'Mallys." She swallowed the bite of sandwich and smiled. "In my mind I can see the inside of O'Mally's Department Store. I have every aisle memorized…the clothing aisles…the shoe aisles…the arts and crafts aisle…the toy aisles…even the 'man' aisles holding tools and fishing stuff." Amanda took another bite of her sandwich. "I can see the snack bar, the pharmacy… and I can even see the baby section."

Sarah felt a gentle smile touch her beautiful face. "Yes… the baby section," she said in a hungry voice.

Amanda smiled back. "O'Mally's is our store, love, and Snow Falls is our little snowy town," she explained. "Someday we're going to spend the entire day in O'Mally's buying nothing but baby clothes, bottles, diapers, food, a baby crib, baby toys, blankets, rattlers." Amanda nearly burst. "Inside of our store, love…our O'Mally's." Amanda took some coffee down. "I know O'Mally's is a simple little department store, but to me, that store is part of my life…my heart. Snow Falls is a part of me…this coffee shop is a part of me…the snow is a part of me." Amanda tossed her eyes at the front door. "That storm outside is simply an old friend stopping by to chat for a bit."

Sarah studied Amanda's sweet, nostalgic eyes. "I love Snow Falls, too," she promised, looking down at her coffee. She grew silent for a minute. "I do miss my life in Los Angeles. When Pete and I teamed up to catch that dirty cop, it felt like I had come home. I know a part of me will always belong to Los Angeles." Sarah raised her eyes and found Amanda. "A part of me will always belong to Snow Falls, too…to the snow. I've come to love the snow, June Bug…love the land." Sarah slowly took a sip of her coffee. "I love O'Mally's just as much as you do. I love the diner and this coffee shop and my cabin…Snow Falls has become a part of my heart."

"Mine, too," Amanda smiled. She gobbled down the rest of her sandwich, washed it down with coffee, and continued. "There will always be a part of this woman that belongs in London, love. You can't take London out of the woman. At times I desperately miss London, but London has changed. The people have changed." Amanda wiped her mouth with a brown napkin and then went for a pile of cinnamon rolls sitting on a second green plate resting on the table. "When my hubby and I left London I was heartbroken, love. I was leaving behind my life and trudging out into the wilderness far, far away from home. I was very depressed and sad, but being close to my son was extremely important to me."

Sarah put her chin in her hand and listened to her sweet friend talk with a tender love in her heart.

"It was O'Mally's Department Store that became a dear friend to me," Amanda continued. "I spent countless hours in that little store…well, not so little…walking up and down the aisles, sitting at the snack bar, listening to the snow fall outside…a woman alone." Amanda began to nibble on her cinnamon roll as her lovely eyes walked back through time. "O'Mally's became my best friend…my only friend, until the blokes in this town started talking to me. But even then, or by then should I say, O'Mally's Department Store and the snow had become two of my dearest friends. Still are. Sure, I complain about the cold, but that's simply my way of having a little toss about."

"You really love O'Mally's, don't you?" Sarah said, watching Amanda's eyes glow with affection.

"More than I can put into words," Amanda confessed. "That store…the snow…are my dearest friends, love. I can't actually explain what I feel every time I walk into O'Mally's. Sure, O'Mally's has basically the same merchandise other stores have, but I feel like the merchandise inside of O'Mally's is somehow different…special…not like merchandise at all, but—"

"Home?" Sarah asked.

Amanda stared at Sarah with wide eyes. "Why…yes, love…that's exactly it—home. O'Mally's is home and everything inside of the store is like…everything inside of your home. Not worldly merchandise but…home."

"I feel the same way." Sarah picked up a cinnamon roll,

studied the delicious pastry, and allowed her mind to walk back through time. "There was a special store I shopped at when I lived in Los Angeles called 'Pages of Time.' The store was a simple, quaint place that was more or less a thrift shop that was full of relics from years gone by. I mostly bought clothes from that store, but sometimes I would come across an item…a book…an old magazine…a toy…that, for whatever reason, spoke to my heart." Sarah took a bite of her cinnamon roll. "That little store became a part of me. And then one day, out of the blue, it was gone."

"Gone?" Amanda asked.

"A comic book store appeared in its place just like that. Well, probably over a week or so. I didn't visit the store every single day." Sarah felt her eyes staring up at a goofy comic book sign with tears in her eyes. "Goodbye, old friend," she whispered and then looked at Amanda. "After that I promised to never let myself become emotionally attached to a store again…until O'Mally's. O'Mally's has become a part of me, June Bug. And…you know what?"

"What?"

"We have enough money now to buy out O'Mally's if Old Man O'Mally ever decides to retire." Sarah smiled.

Amanda rolled her eyes. "That old coot isn't ever going to retire. He'll be a hundred years old and still fussing about me eating up all the kosher hot dogs at the snack bar."

"I know," Sarah said, beaming, forgetting—at least temporarily—about the dark shadow lurking somewhere in a world filled with billions of different minds that were all whispering different tunes; some noble and pure, others dark and horrifying. "I never worry about O'Mally's ever closing. I never worry about losing my old friend."

Amanda picked up her coffee and listened to the storm howl and rage. "You know, love, the notion of someday buying O'Mally's has never once crossed my mind? I would love to own the building O'Mally's is housed in. Sure, I love the name…and would even keep the name…but it's the building I love so much…the atmosphere."

"I wish we were both at O'Mally's right now." Sarah smiled. "I wish we were shopping in the baby section, buying everything you mentioned." Sarah looked down at her cinnamon roll. "June Bug…what does it feel like to be pregnant?"

A gentle whisper of tenderness spread across Amanda's face. "Love," she said in a voice that Sarah had never heard before—a voice only a true mother could possess. "When there is a sweet, innocent child growing in your tummy…a precious little life that is connected to you…only our Lord can give a woman such a gift." Amanda touched her tummy. "When my son was living inside of me, growing, he became a part of my heart forever. Every day I felt his precious little life inside of me…dreaming…giggling…sleeping…clinging to his mommy. Oh, I can't exactly put into words what it feels like to have a sweet little dream growing inside of you…what motherhood feels like." Amanda kept her hand on her tummy. "Real motherhood, not the kind of motherhood that you see today where women don't even want their own unborn child…evil. I'm talking about mothers who treasure their unborn child…nurture that sweet baby for nine sweet months, give birth, and then begin the greatest journey of raising that child inside of your very own heart and soul."

"Try to explain," Sarah begged.

Amanda's eyes glowed with love. "All I can say is that when

a woman becomes pregnant, she receives the greatest gift she will ever know on this earth. An innocent, delicate life…depending on his mommy…feeling that life living inside of you…oh, love…someday you will know yourself, I'm sure of it."

Sarah felt tears begin to well up in her eyes. "Will I? Conrad and I can't become pregnant, Amanda. Yet somehow…I feel my child out there…waiting for me." Sarah allowed her tears to fall. "When your son drives to Snow Falls to visit you," she continued, "I see how you two look at each other. You two share a bond…an eternal bond…that I'm jealous of."

"Oh, love, don't cry."

"How can I not?" Sarah asked. "I see the way your son looks at you, June Bug. I see the love your son has for his mother—a love that is eternal, filled with purity and innocence, truth and…and…completion. Your son completes a part of your very heart, June Bug, that wasn't complete before he was born. You're so very blessed."

"Yes, I am." Amanda rubbed her tummy one last time, then stood up and walked over to Sarah. "Love," she said in a soothing voice, putting her right arm around Sarah, smiling, "my son is my very heartbeat. I love my son as if he were the very air I breathe. Sure, at times my son drives me bonkers with some of the antics he pulls. Sometimes I even wonder if he's sane." Amanda grinned down at Sarah. "But through it all, at the end of each day, when I say my prayers, I know that my son is a beautiful light in this ugly world—a light that I will forever be connected to. Now, with all of that said," Amanda squeezed Sarah's shoulder, "I promise that soon, and very soon, love, you're going to receive the same gift I have."

Sarah looked up into Amanda's loving eyes, wiped her tears, and then placed her head on Amanda's tummy. "Do you really think so?"

Amanda placed a caring, motherly hand down onto Sarah's head. "I know so, love. I pray for you every day. I know my prayers do not go unheard. Be patient."

"Easier said than done," Sarah whispered as more tears fell from her sad eyes. "Listen to me…I sound like a pouty teenage girl."

"You sound like a woman who wants to become a mother," Amanda corrected Sarah as a powerful gust of wind thundered into the front door, nearly tearing the door off its hinges. Amanda jumped. "My, that sounded like a tornado."

Sarah raised her head and looked at the front door. Suddenly her mind was reminded of Lara Wilston. "Wind gusts are expected to reach seventy-five to eighty-five miles per hour," she explained. "I guess that was the storm's way of saying the gusts have arrived."

"I guess," Amanda agreed in a worried voice. As much as she loved the snow, the winds were always a deep concern. "I do hope the tree standing on the north end of my cabin doesn't fall. My hubby trimmed away some of the higher branches, but I always worry that the tree might fall."

"That old tree is pretty strong and has endured many winters," Sarah tried to assure Amanda. She stood up, walked over to the front door, and placed her hand against the strong wood. The storm raced up to the door and began clawing to get inside—clawing to reach Sarah and pull her down into an eternal, dark nightmare. "All we can do is wait out this storm," she told Amanda. "All we can do is…wait."

Amanda joined Sarah at the door. "Too bad O'Mally's isn't open," she tried to joke but failed. "More coffee, love?"

"Why not?" Sarah wiped at the last of her tears, let out a tired breath, and turned away from the front door. "Want to bake a cake?"

"Sure," Amanda replied, forcing a weak smile to her face as the winds screamed and howled, screamed and howled, at the coffee shop. "We can bake a coconut cake if you would like? We have all the needed ingredients."

"Sounds good," Sarah agreed. "I—" The telephone sitting on the front counter cut Sarah off. "That could be Conrad." Sarah rushed to the phone. "Conrad—"

"Hello, Sarah," Lara said, smiling at the other end of the line.

Sarah froze. Her blood cold. The friendly "Lara" she had spoken to days before no longer sounded friendly at all. "Hello, Ms. Wilston."

Lara sat down at a fancy table in a posh coffee shop designed for minds that craved popularity but were in fact clouded with delusional thoughts masquerading as intelligence. "By now you have come to realize that I am not a nurse."

"Yes," Sarah answered in a hard voice.

"Terrific," Lara responded in a voice filled with hunger and violence. "My little play area has allowed you to realize that I'm in control and that I could have and still can kill you at any time of my choosing."

Sarah closed her eyes. The snowman appeared and began laughing at her. The game was on.

Chapter Six

Sarah decided to play "Cop" and ask standard questions in order to—hopefully—loosen Lara's tongue enough to start playing a little manipulation game. "What do you want?"

Amanda grabbed her coffee, eased over to the front counter on silent legs, and listened. Even though Lara was far away, Amanda felt that somehow the killer could sense her presence. "Be tough, Los Angeles," she whispered.

Sarah nodded. "What do you want, Ms. Wilston…and I know that's not your real name."

Lara scanned the coffee shop. Her eyes pulled in nothing but a crowd of kids between the ages of sixteen and twenty; kids who looked as if they were the children of old hippies still sitting in a farmer's field singing "far-out" melodies. One kid —a guy who was skinny enough to be a broom stick—had sideburns so long they nearly pulled his pointy face down to the floor. The kid was wearing what he thought was a cool shirt with a stupid statement written on it. The shirt, the kid assumed, was supposed to impress a real pretty girl who had allowed herself to be real ugly real fast by defending ideas that were enough to make a communist run for the hills. Lara didn't mind the kid, though. The worse the crowd, the better. Why? Because she could speak openly and the mental cases surrounding her would all give her a thumbs-up and a far-out smile.

"In time, Sarah," Lara promised, waving at a dorky waiter buzzing around all the tables and ordering a fancy coffee. The waiter, finding Lara a bit…aged…to be "hip," took the order and wandered off assuming Lara was some college professor who was attempting to relive her popular days.

"You killed Dr. Wester."

Lara removed a black leather jacket, revealing a black sweater (a black that matched her heart) and grinned. "Did I?"

"Yes," Sarah stated, forcing patience and training to her mind. She heard Pete's voice say *A good cop listens more than she talks, kiddo, and thinks smart.* "You killed an innocent woman for no other reason than to play a very sick game." The image of a sweet, caring woman flashed through Sarah's mind followed by deep anger that only a cop could understand. "You're going to spend the rest of your life rotting behind prison bars."

"Is that so?" Lara asked and let out a laugh that sounded like a slithery snake. "Sarah, please, let's not entertain useless dialogue. We are both adults, are we not? You are a cop and I am the villain. We must both portray our roles without wasting priceless seconds throwing useless threats into the air." Lara settled her mind. "My objective is to kill you…that is my long-term objective. My short-term objective is to make you suffer. It's really that simple."

"Yes, I suppose it is," Sarah agreed.

"Of course it is," Lara said in a finalized voice. "Your duty, Sarah, is to try and capture me. But first you must discover what my true identity is, sit around drinking endless cups of coffee trying to understand my game...my mindset, so to speak...and then create a worthless trap."

"You seem to have the game all figured out."

"The rules are simple," Lara pointed out. "Some killers attempt to complicate the rules. Me, I like to keep the game simple while, shall we say, keeping the opposition...busy."

Sarah took a few seconds to run Lara's words into a dusty file room located within her mind. The room was filled with old files that were layered in thick dust; files Sarah had nearly forgotten about. "You want me dead because I've rubbed you the wrong way," she finally spoke. "Somewhere in the seconds of time I've rubbed you the wrong way, right? Sure, it's always that way, Lara." Sarah glanced at Amanda and made a writing motion with her left hand. "Pad and pencil...my office... hurry," she whispered. Amanda nodded and hurried into the kitchen. "Were you recently released from prison? No...you don't have that prison stench in your voice."

"My eyes will never see prison, Sarah, I assure you of that," Lara promised. "I have already promised myself that before a cop ever places handcuffs on me I would terminate my own life. It's that simple." Lara glanced around the coffee shop and spotted the nerdy waiter talking to a silly girl who was pretending she was oh-so-hip and knew every secret the world had to offer. "My game, Sarah...my rules. In the end I win, no matter what."

"I don't call turning into a coward winning," Sarah responded, hoping to push Lara a little. "But I don't really expect anything else," she continued as the storm growled and beat on the front door with icy fists. "All killers are cowards, Lara. They hide in the shadows like cowards and attack. I can't recall one killer I've captured that ever decided to face me out in the open. Why? Because all killers are afraid of facing the truth. You're no different."

Lara felt anger begin to bubble in her cheeks. Sarah was speaking out of line. "Sarah—"

"You're after me because somewhere in your deranged mind you believe your actions are justified," Sarah cut Lara off in a stern tone. "But instead of facing me in a fair fight, you've decided to join the ranks of countless cowards and play a sick, evil game. You're nothing special, Lara. I've dealt with—and destroyed—your kind countless times in the past." Sarah closed her eyes, saw the hideous snowman hissing at her, and drew in a brave breath. "You believe you are unique… brilliant…special. Inside of your diseased mind you believe that you are above the law. You believe that you are smarter than the law and therefore are in complete control while you carry out your evil game. The truth is, Lara, in the end, all killers get caught."

"You think you're so clever, don't you?" Lara hissed at Sarah. "You think you're invincible, don't you? Sure, you do. You think you're the greatest because you managed to capture the Back Alley Killer. Well, let me tell you something, Sarah, you're not as smart as you believe and you're certainly not invisible. And let me warn you: I'm not your run-of-the-mill killer. No, Sarah, I'm someone that is very special…and very much in control of this game. You will learn this truth in the near future. Right now, we have a storm separating us, but the storm can't last forever, now can it? No, when the storm lets up, the game continues. And let me warn you, Sarah, when the game continues, I will begin setting the rules."

Sarah lifted her left hand and touched the bridge of her nose. Rules, games, killers, revenge…all the lunacy was mingled into one ugly color. "I'm not playing your game, Lara."

"Then people will die."

"So be it," Sarah replied, sending a distant hand through the storm that slapped Lara across her face. Lara had expected to control Sarah by threatening to kill again. "Lara, I'm not a cop anymore. I'm retired. You better understand that before you set your…rules," Sarah finished in an insulting voice, deliberately enraging Lara. She needed to see which buttons to push and how far the fuse attached to Lara's mind ran.

Lava began to drip from Lara's eyes. The Back Alley Killer had trained her how to become a monster who preyed on innocent people—and how to manipulate the authorities by throwing their own morality into jeopardy. Murder and conscience equaled two travelers upon life's road that kept a safe distance from one another. And when both eventually mingled together under a dark rock, the killer, Lara was taught, always managed to stick its enemy with a vicious stinger in order to make the police obey. Sarah wasn't playing by the rules. The woman was cutting the stinger off the scorpion with a strange and alien blade that struck a vicious blow to Lara's mind.

"Don't test me," Lara heard her mouth threaten Sarah. "Dr. Wester was simply the tip of the iceberg and—"

"You assume I care?" Sarah snapped, clearly reading Lara's voice. She had managed to knock Lara off balance—but only for a few seconds. It was vital Sarah capitalize on her victory. It was time to play rough. "You know who I am, which means you're probably aware of the books I write," she snapped again. "I've walked in the shadows, too, Lara—for far too long. Do you really believe I care about your victims? After years of being consumed by murder my conscience has become numb. So go play your silly game, but I assure you in the end I will capture you. Why? Because I walk in the shadows, too, Lara, and understand your kind."

Something in Sarah's voice…something deep and strange…sent fear into Lara; a fear Lara had never felt before. Watching an arrogant cop run the talk show circuit in order to brag about capturing the Back Alley Killer had created a lame view of Sarah in Lara's mind. Detective Sarah Garland, in Lara's view—and according to her old man—was nothing more than a stupid cop who had gotten lucky—nothing more and nothing less.

But were the angry words of a killer really true? Had Sarah Garland simply "gotten lucky" and managed to capture one of the deadliest killers to terrorize the state of California? Watching reruns of Sarah speaking to prissy little talk show hosts allowed Lara to believe the woman was nothing more than an arrogant cop seeking two minutes of fame—a cop who had eventually, according to the Back Alley Killer, come to her senses and realized she had become the number one target of a dark mind, and in doing so, had tried to run and hide. Sarah's sudden departure from Los Angeles seemed to confirm the woman had become consumed by fear. Yet, as Lara spoke to Sarah, her ears didn't hear the words of a woman who feared the shadows.

"My kind?" Lara finally asked as if her mouth had been filled with acid. "Sarah, my kind…you will never understand."

You will never win, Sarah, the voice of the hideous snowman wearing a black leather jacket and chewing a candy cane growled through a vicious snarl. *You will never win!* Sarah felt the snowman standing outside in the storm, leaning against the front door, looking up and down the small main street with cruel eyes, searching for a helpless victim. *You will never win, Sarah. Even if you destroy this shadow there'll be more…endless…endless.*

"Prove it," Sarah dared Lara, feeling a cold fear grip her heart. "Prove to me that you're different from every deranged killer I captured." Sarah paused as a strange feeling swept through her. Then, without understanding why, the face of the Back Alley Killer materialized in her troubled mind. "Including the Back Alley Killer," Sarah finished, confused as to why she mentioned a cruel monster that was now dead.

"You think you're smart, don't you!" Lara screamed loud enough to bring attention to herself. A few snotty kids cast impatient glances at Lara—glances that told the woman to clearly shut up or take a hike. Lara looked around at the staring faces and began memorizing every warm body stupid enough to offer insulting glances. If only the snotty kids who wanted to change the world into one giant socialist tumor understood who Lara truly was. Oh, if those diseased minds truly knew…they would begin breathing fear instead of arrogance. And maybe, Lara thought as an invisible venom sipped through her deadly eyes, after disposing of Sarah, she would return to this coffee house and begin killing off every face who had dared to enter her eyes, casting a dark cloud of murder over Anchorage, Alaska. "You were lucky, Sarah…the Back Alley Killer—"

"Is dead!" Sarah hammered into Lara. "The Back Alley

Killer is dead, Lara. Why? Because in the end, every killer ends up in a deep grave." Sarah drew in a deep breath and steadied her mind as Amanda rushed back into the front room carrying a pad of paper and a pencil. "In the end, Lara, good always wins over evil. Why? Because deep inside of a person's heart, there is good." Sarah wasn't sure if the words she had thrown at Lara would cause any harm, but she felt her mind beginning to run low on fuel. The image of the Back Alley Killer that was now stuck behind her eyelids was quickly draining Sarah's mental and emotional desire to fight.

If Sarah had been present in the coffee house, Lara would have openly strangled the woman with her bare hands. "Perhaps the Back Alley Killer isn't dead," she snapped before being able to gain control over her flaring temper. "Perhaps, Sarah, the Back Alley Killer left behind a little surprise for you."

Cold ice began to form inside of Sarah's mind—ice that was quickly turning into prison bars, trapping her in a room of despair and fear. *The Back Alley Killer isn't dead, Sarah!* The snowman laughed as it slithered through the ice bars and began taunting a very frightened woman. *You thought he was dead, didn't you, Sarah…but he isn't!* "The Back Alley Killer was shot dead right before my eyes, Lara," Sarah finally managed to speak. "The monster is dead."

"Is he?" Lara snapped and slammed down her cell phone, abruptly ending the call as more lava dropped from her deadly eyes. "Okay, Sarah, we'll change the rules," she whispered and then slowly stood up like a corpse rising up from a coffin. "We'll change the rules," Lara whispered again and exited the coffee shop, leaving behind a group of people who would continue trying to destroy all that was good in the world.

"Hey…your coffee…lady!" the waiter who had taken Lara's order yelled and then rolled his eyes. "Old bat…stay out!"

Sarah put down the phone with a shaky hand. "What is it, love?" Amanda asked, reading Sarah's eyes. Fear and confusion were flooding into the room. "Love?"

"Why did I mention his name?" Sarah whispered. She threw her eyes toward the front door and then shivered all over. "Why did I mention the Back Alley Killer? The monster is dead, Amanda…you shot him…we saw his body…why did I mention his name?" Sarah closed her eyes, saw the snowman slither away as the ice cage began to melt, and then bowed her head. "The Back Alley Killer isn't dead," she whispered in a voice that gave Amanda the creeps. Outside, the storm continued to scream and howl as it roamed the small town of Snow Falls, Alaska, waiting for a killer to arrive.

Chapter Seven

"Sarah, this woman knows we're trying to have a baby." Conrad's words felt like a hot dagger digging into Sarah's heart. The upset woman looked at her husband with eyes consumed with misery, anger, and worry. Conrad, who was standing beside the front door resembling a frozen watch guard who would never move again, wasn't sure what action to take. The snowstorm had crippled the town—crippled his ability to be a cop.

"I didn't handle the phone call the way I should have," Sarah spoke in a low voice. "I tried to push Lara into a corner. At first it seemed I was accomplishing my goal, but then, for some reason, I mentioned the Back Alley Killer…and everything fell apart."

"The Back Alley Killer is dead, Sarah," Conrad assured his shaken wife. "We need to focus on Lara Wilston. This woman seems to know a great deal about us."

"I agree with Conrad, love," Amanda spoke up, sitting at a coffee table nursing a cup of coffee that seemed strange rather than friendly. "Whoever this Lara Wilston psycho is, she knew you and Conrad were trying to have a baby. Dr. Wester was targeted—"

"As a punishment…a declaration…and to taunt us," Conrad cut in. "Dr. Wester was killed to punish us while Lara Wilston made a statement that she knows our truest desire while taunting us…"

"It does seem that Lara was playing a game she felt in control of," Sarah agreed as her mind walked back through, entered a dark file room, and began investigating the classified file belonging to the Back Alley Killer. "Lara seemed very upset when I informed her the Back Alley Killer was dead…"

"What?" Conrad asked. He carefully checked the lock on the front door and decided it was safe enough to walk to the front counter and join his wife. "What did you say, honey?"

Sarah slowly positioned herself on a brown stool, keeping her eyes facing the front door, and placed her hands down onto her lap. Feeling mentally drained and emotionally unsettled, she allowed her eyes to remain in the dark file room while her mouth spoke to Conrad. "Lara Wilston seemed very upset when I informed her the Back Alley Killer was dead," she spoke again. "Why?"

"I don't—" Conrad began to speak, watching Sarah's eyes wandering around inside of a place that he wasn't allowed to see.

"Lara's response was 'Is he?'" Sarah told Conrad, keeping her voice steady as she plopped down behind a dusty desk inside of her mind and began reviewing the file of a killer. "'Is he?' That's the question Lara left me with. Why?" Sarah frantically began searching through the file in her mind—searching for one single piece of information.

"Sarah, there are many reasons why—" Conrad began to speak.

"Not this time," Sarah informed her husband. "I touched a fragile nerve, Conrad…a nerve that is clearly still exposed to the elements."

Conrad threw a worried eye at Amanda, who put down the cup of coffee she was holding and let out a deep, frightened breath. "You know what Sarah is telling you," she told Conrad, standing up and approaching the front counter. "The Back Alley Killer isn't dead."

"Amanda, you shot the guy dead," Conrad insisted. "I checked the morgue four times before the state got his body. The guy was a cold, dead fish filled with lead when the state took him."

"Amanda killed the body of the Back Alley Killer," Sarah informed Conrad, finally locating the piece of information she needed. "But not his mind…or his heart."

"What do you mean?" Conrad asked as a powerful gust of icy wind nearly tore through the front door. Conrad quickly ran to the door and checked it over. "Wind is getting worse."

"So is this case," Sarah said as the woman inside of her mind held up a single piece of paper and began to read it. "The Back Alley Killer has one child…a daughter."

Conrad froze. Amanda stood very still. "Go on, love," she urged Sarah.

"The daughter of the Back Alley Killer was never located," Sarah continued as she studied the piece of paper her mind had dug up. "Lisa Mandy Wilson…given up for adoption at birth."

"Lisa Mandy Wilson?" Conrad asked as his mind quickly

began playing with the name. "Lisa…Lara…Wilson… Wilston…"

"The child vanished from Sunbeach Elementary School when she was seven years old," Sarah carefully continued with her report. "Eventually, as with most missing person cases, Lisa Wilson was tossed into a filing cabinet and forgotten about, but not before her mother was found dead on a remote Oregon beach. The report I read claimed suicide by drowning was the cause of death…remorse for Lisa Wilson vanishing into thin air."

Conrad pressed his back against the front door. "But?" he asked, reading Sarah's voice.

Sarah kept her mind focused on the piece of paper the woman in her mind was holding. "The Back Alley Killer…we could never tie him to Brenda Wilson's death. The monster didn't begin his killing spree until years later, when Lisa would have been pushing at least thirty. I can't remember the exact year she was born. I always assumed Brenda Wilson hid her daughter and then killed herself before her ex-husband could get to her. It seems my assumption was…wrong."

Conrad felt his heart begin to beat harder and harder. "Are you trying to tell me that Lara Wilston is the daughter of the Back Alley Killer?" he asked Sarah. Mittens, who was asleep in the kitchen, heard Conrad's question and let out a low whine.

"Yes," Sarah answered in a direct voice that left no room for argument. "Lara left me with a simple question…a question that exposed her true identity."

"And now it seems like that monster wants to settle the score, as you Americans say," Amanda added, hugging her arms and shivering all over. "Oh, just the thought of that killer's…residue…slithering around in the snow…creepy. I think I would rather be back at the hot springs trying to figure out how to survive the virus we became infected with…minus the bear, of course."

"We couldn't see the virus that we became infected with, June Bug," Sarah replied, "and we might not be able to see the virus that is currently wanting us dead."

"Us?" Amanda gulped.

"You're the one who shot the Back Alley Killer dead," Sarah explained. "Lara is targeting me first because I was the cop who broke her daddy. But in the end, she will come for the woman who actually shot the monster."

"That's what I was afraid of." Amanda gulped again. "Uh…cinnamon roll, anyone?"

"No thank you, June Bug."

"A refill on my coffee would be good," Conrad told Amanda as he stared at Sarah. "You seem confident."

"I'm not confident. I'm certain," Sarah promised. "Honey, Lara Wilston knows we're trying to have a baby. I'm the reason her daddy is dead. She targeted Dr. Wester as a message—to taunt me." Sarah slowly touched her tender tummy. "Lara was clearly telling me she will never allow me to become a mother…tit for tat."

Anger—a deep, personal anger—that Conrad had never experienced before erupted inside of his heart. "No one is ever going to prevent us from having a baby!" he yelled and then kicked the front door so hard his right foot nearly shattered into thousands of little pieces. "This Lara Wilston…Lisa Wilson…she's going to end up…"

"I know, honey," Sarah promised. She quickly stood up, ran over to Conrad, and hugged him. "Right now, all we can do is wait until this storm passes and then…wait for Lara to show up." Sarah placed her head down onto Conrad's shoulder. "In the meantime, we have time to form a plan. I'm just not certain what kind of plan."

Conrad placed his hand on Sarah's head. "We could block the roads—"

"Lara would come through the woods."

"We could have the State Police set up roadblocks—" Conrad struggled.

"Lara would wait out the roadblocks," Sarah answered. "The State Police can't have year-round roadblocks."

Frustration gripped Conrad's mind. All the man could do —all anyone could do—was wait out the storm and then wait for another storm to arrive; a storm in the form of a killer. "We can leave town as soon as the storm ends," he suggested, despising every word. Running away like a coward wasn't his game. But allowing some deranged killer a free shot at his wife wasn't part of his game, either.

Sarah lifted her head and looked deep into Conrad's eyes. "You know as well as I do running isn't the answer, honey. Lara will keep following us…and we'll always be looking over our shoulder." Sarah shook her head. "Who knows what Lara is capable of? Maybe she might wait until we have a baby…if we ever do…and strike then. There's no telling how far I pushed her over the edge."

"So we sit tight and wait for an unseen killer to attack?" Conrad asked in a desperate voice and then gently placed his hands down onto Sarah's tummy. "I want our baby," he begged as a tear dripped from his eye. "Sarah, I…I know I…I admit I'm scared to be a daddy, but at night, when we're lying in bed, I lie there for hours dreaming of our child…what he or she might look like. Things we'll do together as a family…holidays…the works."

Seeing Conrad's tear broke Sarah's heart. She quickly lifted her hand and wiped at the tear. "I know, honey. I wake up and find you awake…I know what you're thinking about."

Conrad struggled to fight back his tears. "I want to be a daddy," he told Sarah in a shaky voice. "I want to have baby spit-up all over my clothes. I want to go to work smelling like baby food. I want to warm baby bottles and do the three o'clock morning feedings. I want…I want…" A stream of tears began to flow from Conrad's eyes. "Sometimes people forget that pregnancy involves the dad, too…that men want to be daddies…have families…"

"Oh, honey," Sarah whispered, wiping at her husband's tears. She looked deep into his broken eyes. "I—"

"I want us to be a family…you, me, and the baby makes three," Conrad explained and then let out a heavy breath. "The thought of some monster destroying my life…taking you and the baby away…" Conrad shook his head. "I've been playing it cool, Sarah. When you encountered trouble in Michigan I had to stand back and let you handle that trouble your way. Why? Because I've been scared…really scared…of becoming overprotective. Before we got married you were a cop. You still are a cop…and I respect that. I can't throw you into a plastic bubble and keep you there, but, Sarah, this is the last straw. No more. I can't play it cool anymore. It's killing me."

"Okay, honey," Sarah promised, "you can place me into a plastic bubble. I won't object."

"I wish I could." Conrad sighed, took Sarah's soft hands into his own, and continued. "Right now, I need a partner to help protect my wife. I need Sarah the cop to protect Sarah my wife. Can you understand that?"

"Yes," Sarah whispered, feeling a pure and tender love resonating from Conrad—a love she had once desired from her first husband; a love that was never born into existence. "You need me to be a cop right now."

"That's the only way our baby is going to survive this nightmare," Conrad answered Sarah and then gently kissed her lips. "Sarah, I'm just a plain New York cop. You're the smart one—"

"Don't believe that—"

"I'm speaking the truth," Conrad insisted. "Your detective skills are sharper than mine. I'm not saying I'm a slouched cop sitting on a curb, but compared to you…" Conrad shook his head. "Sarah, I read the case files on the Back Alley Killer. I would have never caught that monster."

"Conrad, if it hadn't been for Pete, I would have never caught the Back Alley Killer, either."

"I'm not so sure that's true," Conrad objected. "According to Pete, he did offer a little help, but he assured me you would have bounced back onto the right trail sooner or later."

"Conrad—"

"Honey, listen," Conrad begged, "all I'm trying to say is that if this Lara Wilston woman is the daughter of the Back Alley Killer, that means we're dealing with a serious killer and not just some lame gas station bum who took a life for a twenty-dollar bill." Conrad walked Sarah over to a coffee table and sat down. "Lara Wilston knows we were trying to have a baby and killed Dr. Wester as a way to get a sick, punishing message to us real quick. In my view, her target is our… baby…and so help me…"

Sarah sat down across from Conrad. "Okay," she said, forcing her voice to become strong again as she closed off the file room in her mind. "Amanda, honey, can we have some more coffee? It's going to be a very long night and we have a lot of thinking to do."

Conrad raised his head, studied Sarah's eyes, and then looked at Amanda. "Might as well bring out some sandwiches, too, if you don't mind. I'm getting hungry."

"What do I look like?" Amanda fussed at Conrad. "A waitress?"

"Plain…no mayonnaise," Conrad told Amanda.

"Plain…always plain," Amanda griped. "This bloke wouldn't know how to eat a sandwich right if his life depended on it."

Sarah watched Amanda walk into the kitchen fussing up a storm. "Amanda's life is in danger, too," she confessed in a deeply worried voice. "Conrad, that woman means more to me than…she's part of my heart. I couldn't stand to lose her. I think…well, I would go insane if I lost Amanda."

"No one is going to die," Conrad promised.

Sarah kept her eyes on the kitchen door. "Excuse me for a minute," she said in a quick voice. She jumped to her feet, ran into the kitchen, and gave Amanda a tight hug. "I love you, June Bug."

Amanda, feeling a bit shocked, hugged Sarah back. "I love you, too," she promised. "What brought this sudden emotional dance on?"

Sarah placed her hands on Amanda's shoulders. "Shoot first…no hesitation," she ordered in a stern voice. "And you don't leave my eyesight from this point forward, is that clear?"

Amanda read Sarah's worried eyes and nodded. "Shoot

first…I understand," she promised, hugging Sarah, and then pointed at the refrigerator. "I guess we're both making more coffee and sandwiches, right, love?"

Sarah listened to the storm bang on the back door and then found Mittens with her eyes. The dog was lying close to the back door asleep but yet somehow still keeping guard. "Right," she told Amanda. She popped her head into the front room and told Conrad what she was doing.

It was going to be a very long night.

Chapter Eight

Sarah startled awake. A baby was crying. The sound was coming from far away, floating down a dimly lit tunnel filled with fog. Feeling confused and disoriented, Sarah slowly climbed out of a baby's crib and stepped down onto…snow? Yes, the ground was covered in thick, freezing snow. "Snow?" Sarah asked, looking down at her bare feet and wondering why the freezing snow wasn't turning her feet into two ice blocks. That's when she realized that her body was covered in a pink bathrobe that was no match for the howling snowstorm racing back and forth in front of the tunnel, yet the bathrobe seemed to be sufficient enough to keep her warm. "Snow?"

The baby's crying floated down the tunnel again, reaching Sarah's ears the way a desperate child struggles to cross a busy highway in order to find his or her way home. "Hold on…I'm coming…mommy's coming," Sarah whispered, still feeling disoriented. Where was she? What was the tunnel? Why did the tunnel have fog inside of it? Why was it snowing? Sarah walked her confused eyes around the storm but only saw more snow…snow that seemed to stretch for hundreds of miles, covering a flat, bare land. Unable to understand where she was, Sarah focused back on the tunnel. It seemed to be made of some type of…gray clouds? Yes, gray clouds. But why was a tunnel made of gray clouds? And why was a baby inside the tunnel? Sarah wasn't sure. All she knew—or rather felt—was that the baby inside the tunnel was her child.

"Hold on…mommy's coming."

Sarah glanced around at the snow once again and began walking through the deep snow toward the tunnel. As she did, a strange feeling crashed into her body. Suddenly her legs began to feel as if they weighed a million pounds…then her arms…and then her entire body as a whole. "Hold on… mommy's coming," Sarah grunted as she struggled to walk through the snow. "Mommy's coming…hold on." The sweet, innocent cries of the baby continued to float down the tunnel and whisper into Sarah's frantic ears. "Mommy's coming!"

"Never!" a hideous voice screamed.

"Huh?" Sarah managed to barely turn her head and peer off to her right side as a strong gust of wind grabbed her blonde hair. Her terrified eyes didn't immediately spot anyone or anything. But then a strange, alien bump began to form in the snow…slowly at first, like a balloon being filled with drips of air. Sarah watched the bump grow. After what seemed like an hour or more, even though mere minutes had passed, the progress of the bump began to accelerate. Suddenly the bump began to grow faster and faster…growing larger and larger… until the bump grew into the size of a human being. And then, without any warning, the bump exploded. Snow went bursting into the air—only the snow was black rather than white—striking Sarah in her face; some snow struck Sarah's mouth, tasting like rotted screams. Sarah watched in horror as a hideous snowman wearing a black leather jacket appeared chewing a candy cane.

"You!" she screamed.

"Me!" The snowman grinned and then hissed at Sarah as it began to slither toward her like a cobra snake studying its victim. To Sarah's horror, the snowman slithered past her and positioned itself in front of the tunnel. "You will never get to the baby, Sarah! Never!" it hollered.

"No!" Sarah tried to reach her hands up into the air in order to fight but couldn't. Her legs and arms were slowly turning into ice…only the ice seemed to be some type of clear ooze. "No, leave my baby alone, you monster!"

"You created me, Sarah," the snowman hissed and then offered a hideous grin. "You created me. I'm alive because of you."

"No!"

"Oh yes," the snowman continued as it tossed a dangerous eye into the tunnel. "Sarah, you created me, and I'll never go away. I'll always haunt you."

Sarah watched in agony as her arms and legs became covered with the icy, clear ooze. It was now impossible to move. "What do you want from me?" she cried.

"You know, Sarah…you've always known," the snowman growled. "I want your sanity. That's why you created me, right? I represent everything you fear."

Sarah threw her eyes at the tunnel. The baby—her baby—was no longer crying. "You—"

"Murder, Sarah," the snowman spat. "How many murders did your eyes see…did you take home with you at night… dream of? The violence…the darkness, Sarah…attached itself to your heart…and you became afraid, didn't you? Yes, you did. That's why you created me. You had to give a face to your nightmares."

"Go away!"

"Never!" the snowman hollered, taking another candy cane out of the right pocket of the leather jacket and tossing it into his snarling mouth. "You didn't have the guts to give me a real face, did you, Sarah? So you created a stupid snowman. But inside of the snowman all the insanity lived, right? Oh yes, I know."

Sarah fell silent and stared at the hideous snowman. The snowman stared back for a while and then looked back into the tunnel. "Leave my baby alone," Sarah said.

"When your first husband divorced you, Sarah," the snowman hissed, "you could have stayed in Los Angeles and continued your work as a homicide detective, but you were too afraid. You needed an excuse to run…and your divorce was the perfect excuse."

"I was never afraid!"

"Oh yes you were!" the snowman growled, returning its red, glowing eyes to Sarah and hissing at her. "You became afraid after you realized the monster you were truly fighting…but by then it was too late, wasn't it? Oh yes, you became a victim, didn't you? And in order to remain sane you kept doing your job, right? Sure. Keep your enemy in sight, right? As long as you solved murders you would never become someone in a body bag. The fear, Sarah, captured you."

"Leave me——"

The snowman tossed a frozen claw at the tunnel. "And you think you can become a mother living in fear?" he taunted.

"Every night in your dreams you run from me and every day you try to forget me. Impossible."

"I'm…not afraid of you," Sarah tried to yell but her shaky voice caused her words to find disaster rather than victory. She dropped her eyes down onto the snow and let out a miserable moan. "I'm not afraid…"

"Yes, you are!" the snowman insisted. "You were always afraid!"

Sarah kept her head bowed as tears began dropping from her eyes. She watched as each tear struck the snow. "What?" she asked, watching each spot her tears struck begin to glow. The snowman saw this and let out a vicious howl. Sarah snatched her head up and saw the snowman begin backing away from the tunnel.

"You will never win!" the snowman howled. "You can never become a mother as long as I am alive…and Lara Wilston will kill you, Sarah. She's going to seal off this tunnel forever!" The snowman threw his icy claws at the tunnel.

Sarah looked at the tunnel as tears continued to drop from her eyes. "Mommy was afraid…so afraid…" she confessed, feeling her words float into the tunnel and somehow manage to reach the ears of her child. "Mommy was always so afraid… she is still afraid…and she's so sorry for creating a monster…"

The snowman watched in horror as Sarah's tears began forming a pool in the snow. The pool, which was nearly blinding to look at, began to form into a man. "Get back!" the snowman hissed and backed farther away from Sarah. "Get back! This isn't your fight!"

The bright glowing pool continued to form into a man. Minutes later Conrad stepped out of the light wearing an armored suit with only his face showing. "I'm here, Sarah,"

Conrad promised and then pointed a sharp sword at the snowman. "Away with you!"

"This isn't your fight," the snowman hissed at Conrad. "You can run me off, but I'll be back…I can't die because I represent fear!"

"Conrad?" Sarah asked in a confused voice, staring at a man who had the voice of her husband but the face of a strange man who seemed to belong in the year 1512. The man had a long beard and a hard, stone-like face that was scarred with war—a face that held raw courage that was rare to see in the days Sarah was living in.

"Be gone with you!" Conrad ordered the snowman in a voice that was preparing to attack.

The snowman, realizing Conrad was about to attack, let out a vicious hiss. "I'll be back for her!" it threatened and then began sinking down into the snow, melting in a puddle of clear ooze. Seconds later the clear ooze holding Sarah captive began to melt, dripping off her arms and legs like grease.

Sarah watched the ooze melt off her arms and legs and then tried to move. "I can move!" she screamed and started to run for the tunnel. As she did, heavy, thick bars made of ice formed over the entrance. "No!" Sarah cried as she reached the tunnel. "Conrad, help me!"

Conrad ran to the tunnel, ordered Sarah to stand back, and began striking the ice bars with his sword. The bars were too strong. "It's no use…I can't get through!" Conrad yelled in a helpless voice.

Sarah began trying to pull the ice bars apart as the sound of the crying, sweet baby filled her ears. "Hold on, mommy's coming…" Sarah promised as tears streamed from her desperate eyes. "Mommy hears you. Mommy's coming." Sarah continued to yank on the ice bars and Conrad backed away and melted down into the snow. "Mommy's coming…" Sarah screamed as the sound of her baby suddenly grew very silent. "No…keep crying…mommy's coming…"

Suddenly a hand grabbed Sarah's shoulder. Sarah swung around and saw Amanda. "Amanda?"

"Wake up…honey…wake up…you're having a nightmare," Amanda begged and then burst into a ball of snow. Sarah stared at the snow with terrified eyes and then… her eyes slowly opened up…and there was Amanda's face again. "Wake up, honey…wake up…"

"Amanda?" Sarah whispered, feeling a strange sense of reality begin to overtake her tormented mind. "Amanda?"

"Yes, love, it's me," Amanda promised. "Goodness, were you ever having a doozy of a nightmare."

"A nightmare?"

"Who can blame you after sleeping in this lousy place," Amanda complained. "These cots aren't exactly a dream to sleep on."

"Cots?" Sarah took her hands and touched the bed she was sleeping on. The bed felt strange…and very uncomfortable. "What is this?" Sarah managed to lean up and look down. She was lying on top of a brown blanket that was covering an old army cot Andrew had put into the three holding cells inside the jail. "Oh…that's right," she said and began rubbing her eyes. "I fell asleep early this morning in this cell."

Amanda plopped down onto the cot and wrapped a brown blanket around her shoulders. "You were having some nightmare. I heard you all the way over in the next cell," she explained in a sleepy voice.

"I…guess," Sarah responded, still hearing the sound of her

crying baby resonating inside of her heart rather than ears. "Where is Conrad?"

"In his office." Amanda yawned, shook her head, and struggled to wake her mind up. "It's nearly noon. We all fell asleep around five this morning."

Sarah stopped rubbing her eyes, raised her head, and focused on Amanda's tired face. "Did we accomplish anything?"

"Afraid not," Amanda sighed. "You, me, and Conrad paced around the coffee shop all night trying to create a plan. All we ended up doing was wearing our legs down."

"I remember," Sarah told Amanda, letting out her own sigh, and then stood up. As she did, the storm outside greeted her ears. "The storm—"

"Worse than yesterday," Amanda informed Sarah. "I'm afraid we might be looking at another whiteout…like the one on the night we had to crawl through that oversized sewer pipe to reach the home of those three crazy old ladies." Amanda tightened the blanket around her shoulders, stood up, and looked around the small cell. "We could lock ourselves in this cell, or go hide in that oversized sewer pipe?"

"I'm tempted," Sarah told Amanda as the dream she had been held captive in howled inside the tunnels of her heart, sending choruses of misery into her mind. "I guess I'll go get a cup of coffee and go see what Conrad is doing."

"I'll come with you, love." Amanda grabbed Sarah's hand and walked her out of the cell, down a small wooden hallway, into the front room, and over to a coffee station area. "Oh, someone made a fresh pot of coffee and put out donuts," she said, beaming.

"That would be me," Conrad said, leaning against the door leading into Andrew's office.

Sarah spun around, spotted Conrad, and tried to smile. "Did you sleep any?"

"A couple of hours," Conrad confessed. "I spent a few hours on the phone with Pete."

Sarah's heart dropped. "Conrad, we decided not to involve Pete," she stated in a troubled voice. "You know Pete will catch the first flight to Alaska—"

"I know," Conrad cut his wife off with a caring voice. "But I needed help, Sarah," he continued. "You see, as I was dozing off on the floor next to you an idea struck me."

"An idea?" Sarah asked.

Conrad walked over to Sarah and sat her down behind one of the four desks sitting in the front room. "Look, honey, this Lara Wilston has to be using either cash or a credit or bank card. Now, it's possible she may be using cash—"

"Or stolen credit cards," Sarah pointed out.

"Maybe," Conrad nodded, "but—"

"And I doubt Lara Wilston, who apparently is Lisa Wilson, is carrying around a bank or credit card in her real name, Conrad."

"True," Conrad agreed, "but that doesn't mean I can't run down every female name that starts with L and ends with W, right?"

Sarah stared at Conrad. "Conrad—"

"And narrow down my search to Los Angeles," Conrad continued. "I know it's a stretch, Sarah, but right now we have nothing to go on. Besides," Conrad said, pausing to ask Amanda for a cup of coffee, "I just got off the phone with Detective Eastbrook…he's kicking at empty alleys right now."

"What did Pete say?" Sarah dared to ask.

"Besides wanting to stick your head in a toilet for not telling him about Lara Wilston?" Conrad asked.

"Yes." Sarah winced.

Conrad patted Sarah's soft hands. "Honey, he said he won't sleep a wink until he's run every woman with the initials L.W.," he explained and then added: "Pete also wants you to call him."

Sarah winced again. After her nightmare she didn't feel like being yelled at by Pete…but what choice did she have? It was going to be a long day. But what Sarah didn't know was that Conrad's idea would end up throwing a piece of gold into the fight—a piece of gold that would help her destroy Lara Wilston—or so Sarah hoped.

Chapter Nine

Pete logged onto an old dinosaur computer sitting on his desk with tired fingers. "Okay, Jim, let's see what you sent me," he mumbled under his breath while holding a half-smoked cigar in his mouth; a mouth scented with Chinese food and coffee. From an outsider's view, Pete resembled an old 1940s detective wearing a white button-up shirt with gray suspenders. From Pete's point of view, he looked like a retired cop who was worried sick. Lara Wilston had to be the daughter of the Back Alley Killer.

"Come on, come on," Pete fussed at his computer as he tried to jump onto the internet and log onto a secure police site that, technically, Pete was banned from; Jim Wallace had slipped Pete a secret password under the rug. "I don't have time to dilly dally." Pete knew talking to an inanimate object was pointless, but he still fussed at the computer anyway in order to vent. Finally, the internet popped up. Pete quickly went to a "Data and Research" site (the "Police site," as Pete called it) and logged on with the password Jim had slipped him. "Okay…let's go to records…"

As Pete hammered on the gray keyboard sitting on his desk, a hard hand knocked on his office door. Pete lifted a set of cautious eyes, grabbed a Glock 17 from a shoulder holster he had worn for years and years, and yelled: "Who is it?"

"Jim!"

Pete lowered his gun and shook his head. "Stop being jumpy," he snapped at himself and then told Jim to enter his office.

A short, plump little man who could have been mistaken for a miniature Jim Reeves burst into Pete's office as if he were on fire. "Pete—"

"I'm logged into the police site right now, Jim…searching for the file—"

"Forget that," Jim barked. He hurried across a messy office that fit well with a retired cop and snatched a brown folder out from the gray trench coat he was wearing. "I found her!"

Pete stared up at Jim with careful eyes. Sure, Jim resembled a miniature Jim Reeves who belonged in a 1950s sitcom, but the man was a clever cop who had helped solve many difficult cases; well, clever when it came to computers. When it came to people…mostly women…the poor guy fell flat. Jim had not been on a date in over two years; at the age of sixty, that wasn't good. "You found Lara Wilston?"

"I believe so. Look in the folder," Jim barked again in an excited voice. He looked down at Pete's desk, spotted a half-eaten box of Chinese noodles, and helped himself. "Lisa Wilson, right?" he asked.

"Huh?" Pete asked.

"Lisa Wilson…that was the name of the little girl who went missing, right?"

"Yeah," Pete confirmed, watching Jim gobble down his Chinese food.

"Lara Wilston…" Jim said through a mouth full of noodles.

Pete felt frustration rise in his cheeks. "Jim, get to the point!" he snapped.

"Math," Jim explained. "The 'A' and the 'R' replaced the 'I' and the 'S'…Lara…Lisa. And a 'T' was added to the name Wilson. So I decided to do a little numbers game and play around." Jim shoved more noodles into his mouth. The letter 'A' equals 1. The letter 'R' equals 13 and the letter 'T' equals 15."

"Yeah, so?" Pete asked and waited for Jim to continue.

"A total of twenty-nine," Jim explained as he sat down on the edge of Pete's desk. "At first I couldn't find any real importance to that number, but my mind kept falling back to the letters." Jim polished off the noodles and tossed the empty box into a wooden wastebasket perched beside Pete's desk. "The letters 'A', 'R', and 'T' were new. But what struck me the most was the last name…why only add the letter 'T'? So I focused on the number fifteen." Jim locked eyes with Pete. "Does that number ring a bell?"

Pete nodded. "The Back Alley Killer murdered fifteen people before Sarah caught him…well, almost fifteen. Sarah managed to save the fourteenth victim…by skill or luck…who knows? She put a bullet in the Back Alley Killer's shoulder before he killed his victim. The guy managed to escape, though. Jim, I always believed it was that bullet that made the monster lose his stride. Who knows? All I do know is that he managed to come back at Sarah like a raging bull. He killed his next victim out of anger, and that was a fatal mistake and…" Pete paused. Why was he running his mouth to Jim instead of letting his friend get on with the business at hand? "Sorry, Jim…go on."

Jim pulled a cigar out of his trench coat and asked Pete for a match. "Okay, Pete, the name Lara…the two middle numbers…represent the first and thirteenth victims. There was no fourteenth victim and the Back Alley Killer managed to slay one more victim…in order, the victim would be number fifteen. Of course," Jim emphasized, "I could have been way off base, but I ran with it."

Pete lit a match and placed it up to Jim's cigar.

"So I did some digging on victims 1, 13, and 15….but before I go any farther, let me point out that the letter 'T' is added to the last name, separate from the letters 'A' and 'R'… Sarah severed victim 13 from victim 15, allowing victim 14 to serve as kinda a divide."

Pete nodded again. "Okay, go on, Jim."

Jim puffed on his cigar. "Victim 1 was a male. Victim 13 was a female. Victim 14 would have been a female, but victim 15 was a female," Jim explained. "Male…female…female… mom, dad, and daughter? I wasn't sure. I dug into each case file and found out that each victim was childless. Thank goodness for that. However, when I checked each victim's social security number, I noticed a patten of numbers."

"Jim, you're the math whiz, not me. Please get to the point," Pete pleaded.

"Each social security number, the first and the last number, represented a letter…and each letter was connected to the first and last name of each victim. Coincidence? No sir. Looks like the Back Alley Killer likes math, too."

"I'm all ears."

Jim grinned. "I put the numbers 1, 13, and 15 into the system and started to run social security numbers that had those numbers. I came up blank…real bummer for a man my age. But then I remembered that the new banking system that was rolled out a few years back required a four-digit PIN and a—"

"Fifth security digit that has to be used when out of state," Pete finished for Jim as his mind began to play catch-up.

"Exactly!" Jim beamed. "I have a friend who works at the National Bank downtown…and, well, Pete, he owed me a favor." Jim took a second to work on his cigar. "Long story short, we're looking for a woman named Natalie Emma Jones…who, at the age of twenty, had her name legally changed from Lisa Mandy Wilson."

"Jim, you're a genius!"

Jim blushed at the compliment. "Don't buy me a box of cigars until the killer is caught," he told Pete. "Natalie Emma Jones has been using her bank card quite a bit…are you ready…in—"

"Alaska!"

"In Alaska," Jim confirmed. "The woman is currently registered at the Holiday Inn and Suites."

Pete could barely believe his ears. "I'm calling Alaska right now."

"Hold on," Jim warned. "Pete, Lisa Mandy Wilson, aka Natalie Emma Jones, is loaded, and I mean loaded. We're talking over twenty million dollars. If the police go racing at her without any evidence, you know the deal, Pete, all that dough will be used to eat up every cop with expensive lawsuits." Jim worked on his cigar a second and then asked: "What evidence do we have so far?"

Pete leaned back in an old leather chair. "None, Jim… none whatsoever."

"At least we now have a face," Jim replied and nodded at the folder. "Open the folder."

Pete felt a bolt of electricity surge through him. He snatched the folder open and picked up a head shot of a beautiful—nearly breathtaking—young woman. "This is Natalie Jones?"

"At the age of twenty-two." Jim nodded. "Natalie Jones was a popular model back in her day. At the age of thirty-one she dropped off the modeling scene and started a magazine that belly-flopped. She returned to Los Angeles shortly after the Back Alley Killer started…killing." Jim looked at his cigar. "Pete, this woman stayed in Los Angeles the entire time. She didn't even leave Los Angeles when the Back Alley Killer went to Alaska to try and kill Sarah."

"Personal vendetta," Pete confirmed.

"Maybe…sure seems that way." Jim rubbed the back of his neck. "I still have a long night ahead of me, Pete, but for now, it seems like daddy's little girl came home to help him carry out the killings. I'm still having my friend at the bank run all of Natalie's financial records for the last twenty-three years. Who knows what we will come up with?"

Pete studied the face of Emma Jones…who was once Lisa Wilson…who was now going by the name Lara Wilston. "How'd she get all that money?"

"Married an old geezer who was loaded," Jim replied.

"Money can help a person change their entire life on paper," Pete said aloud, speaking mostly to himself. "If we let this killer slip through our fingers, she'll vanish."

"Unless we have evidence to pin on Emma Jones…yeah,

she will," Jim agreed. "Lara Wilston is fake name that can go up in smoke. Lisa Wilson is a name that has been destroyed, Pete. We have to catch Natalie red-handed or we lose."

"At least the fake name Natalie used allowed you to use your brain and track down the truth." Pete looked at Jim. "Jim, you're a real friend, and I swear you're one of the smartest men alive. Thanks for all your help."

Jim blushed again. "I like to play Sudoku," he replied in a humble voice.

"I would have never made the connections you did, Jim."

"I was a big fan of Sherlock Holmes when I was a kid," Jim explained, putting out his cigar in a tin ashtray and standing up. "Pete, the ball is in your court now. I'll keep the lamp lit at my end and let you know what movements I see on Natalie's financial records. If I see anything important, I'll call you."

"At least we know the woman is still in Anchorage—"

Before Pete could finish his sentence, a cell phone resting in the right pocket of Jim's trench coat rang. Jim pulled it out and checked the caller. "It's my friend from the bank…could be important," he told Pete and answered the call. "Yeah, Ryan, what do you have?"

A sixty-two-year-old man who was earning a large belly tapped a pen against a glowing computer screen. "Your person of interest has checked out of the Holiday Inn and Suites," he told Jim. "That was about three hours ago. I'm staring at a recent transaction…looks like your person of interest bought a brand new truck, a hauling trailer, and a snowmobile." Ryan stopped tapping the screen. "Last transaction was at a gas station located in the northern part of Anchorage."

"She's on the move," Jim barked at Pete. "Ryan—"

Ryan heard steps outside of his office door. "I'm going silent," he whispered and ended the call just as a snotty woman entered his office and began complaining about a set of reports that were late.

Jim tossed his phone down. "You better call Sarah, Pete."

Pete grabbed his phone and called the phone in Andrew's office since all cell phone reception was down due to the storm. Conrad picked up on the third ring. "It's Pete, Conrad," he said. "Our snake is on the move toward your location. Bought a truck, a hauling trailer, and a snowmobile and headed out of town."

Conrad threw his eyes at Sarah, who was standing at the office window looking out at the storm. "Lara is on the move," he explained in a calm but worried voice.

Sarah turned away from the window and locked eyes with Conrad. "Is that Pete?" Conrad nodded. Sarah drew in a deep breath, walked over to the desk, and took the phone. "Hey, Pete—"

"I'll deal with you later, kiddo," Pete nearly bit Sarah's head off. "You know better than to hold information from me. And before you say anything, I know you were only trying to protect me, I get that…but we're cops!" Pete hit his desk with a hard hand. "We're partners, you green behind the ears… runt!"

Sarah winced. Pete was furious. "Pete—"

"Don't Pete me!" Pete yelled and hit his desk again. "We're partners, Sarah…do you understand that? Can you get that piece of information stuck in that thick head of yours?" Pete shook his head. "Sometimes I wonder if you have marshmallows for a brain."

Sarah winced again. "Pete—"

Pete spit his cigar out. "Listen here…Detective," he snapped, "our killer is now on the move and thanks to Jim Wallace we now know who our killer is…we have a positive lock. But do you care? Nah…you didn't even care to bother and let me know the daughter of one of the deadliest killers we have ever tangled with was hunting you down!" Pete shot to his feet. "No, you listen to me and listen carefully. From this point forward you better realize I mean business. If you ever, and I mean ever, withhold information from me again I'm going to…you would be better off tangling with a grizzly bear, is that clear!"

"Yes, Pete, loud and clear." Sarah winced for a third time.

Pete felt his cheeks burning. "Natalie Emma Jones…Lisa Mandy Wilson changed her name to Natalie Emma Jones when she was twenty years old. Natalie married a rich geezer… she's loaded, has enough money to run us in circles. I'll explain how Jim locked onto her later after my brain has had time to digest his methods." Pete slowly sat back down. "I'm going to fax you a photo of Natalie Emma Jones, Detective."

"Thank you, Pete." Sarah bit down on her lower lip and waited for Pete to bark again. When Pete fell silent, Sarah knew the storm had passed—one storm, at least; a new storm was approaching.

Chapter Ten

"Natalie Emma Jones?" Conrad said as he took a drink of coffee. "Well, at least we have a positive name. That's something."

"Isn't knowing Lara Wilston's real name something, love?" Amanda asked Sarah.

"It depends," Sarah confessed as she nibbled on a plain donut. For whatever reason she felt a little nauseous. Sarah marked the uneasy feeling in her stomach as due to drinking far too much coffee and eating far too little along with stress. "We do have a name, but so what? Lara is still heading our way."

"But we have a face," Amanda insisted.

"The face of a young model," Sarah pointed out, walking over to the window in Conrad's office and peeking out at the snow-covered street. "Lara could have—and most likely has—altered her appearance, June Bug," she said, feeling more nauseous by the second. "I—" Sarah dropped her eyes down to the donut she was nibbling on. Suddenly the donut appeared revolting instead of tempting. "I—" She tried to speak again and then, without any warning, threw down the donut, charged out of Conrad's office, and ran to the nearest bathroom and began throwing up.

Alarmed by Sarah's sudden departure, Conrad and Amanda hurried after her. "Sarah!" Conrad called out. "Sarah!"

"Stay here," Amanda ordered Conrad and rushed into the ladies' bathroom—a small, cramped little wooden room holding a single toilet. Sarah was on her knees vomiting into the toilet. "Oh my…" Amanda whispered as she closed the bathroom door.

"Must…be the donuts," Sarah tried to speak as she vomited.

Amanda quickly wet a paper towel and handed it to Sarah. "For your mouth, love."

Sarah took the paper towel and wiped at her mouth as her stomach slowly began to settle. "Must be the donuts. I haven't eaten anything else today."

Amanda squatted down and looked deeply into Sarah's eyes. "If the donuts are the culprits, love, then why aren't I sick…or Conrad?" she asked as the sweetest smile Sarah had ever seen in her life formed across Amanda's beautiful face.

"What are you talking about?" Sarah asked in a confused voice.

Amanda held out a gentle hand and touched Sarah's belly. "Morning sickness…maybe?"

"Morning sickness…but we're already into the afternoon hours…" Sarah stared into Amanda's glowing eyes. "June Bug, there's no way I can be pregnant. As much as I want…desire… to be pregnant, there is simply no possible way."

"Oh?" Amanda asked as her smile grew wider. "I've been

praying my heart out…God answers prayers the same today as He did hundreds of years go. Miracles still happen every day in this world." Amanda helped Sarah stand up. "I was reading…oh…last week, I suppose…about a seven-year-old boy who had fallen into an icy river and drowned. Hours later, when all hope was lost, the little boy…simply woke up." Amanda smiled into Sarah's eyes. "Miracles happen every day, love."

"But…I…" Sarah stared into Amanda's eyes. "All those tests…the doctors…Dr. Wester…the test showed negative… Dr. Wester…"

"What doctors don't understand is that God is in control. Remember Rachel? She was barren while Leah had children… and then God remembered Rachel and she had two sons," Amanda explained. "I think we need to locate a pregnancy test kit as soon as possible."

Sarah began to tremble all over. Was she really pregnant? "But…my dream…my fear?" she asked in a confused voice. "I felt that my dream was telling me I would never become pregnant until I killed the snowman."

"Let's focus on your oven for right now," Amanda nearly cried and hugged Sarah. "I need to locate a pregnancy—"

"My purse…Conrad's office…I…out of desperation I always keep one in my purse."

"Don't move an inch!" Amanda yelled. She burst out of the bathroom, ordered Conrad to stand back, and made tracks. A few minutes later, she returned with a pregnancy testing kit and burst back into the bathroom, leaving a confused Conrad standing out in the hallway with a scared expression on his face. "Here it is, love…let's hurry…oh, this is so exciting!"

Sarah stared at the pregnancy testing kit as if the kit were some type of strange and alien life form instead of an object she was very familiar with. "I..." Sarah tried to speak but failed. Instead, she reached out a scared hand, took the kit from Amanda, asked to be left alone, and said a desperate prayer.

"What's going on?" Conrad demanded once Amanda left the bathroom.

"You'll see, you silly bloke." Amanda smiled from ear to ear. "Right now, we need to pray."

"Pray?"

"Pray." Amanda bowed her head and began to pray. Conrad, more confused than ever, didn't know what to pray for. He bowed his head and began praying for the strength to understand what was happening with his wife.

Five minutes passed...and then ten. And right when Amanda was preparing to knock on the bathroom door, the door slowly opened like a prison door finally being destroyed. Sarah appeared holding a plastic pregnancy test result dish. Tears—warm, joyous tears—were flowing from her eyes. "Conrad...I...you..." she tried to speak through her tears but failed. "Here."

Conrad watched Sarah hold out the result dish. "Sarah?" he asked, barely able to speak himself. "I...you mean..."

"The suspense is killing me!" Amanda screamed, and, with excited hands, took the result dish from Sarah. "It's blue!" she hollered and then nearly fainted. "Conrad...blue...blue... blue...there's not red...the two lines are both blue!" Amanda began jumping up and down. "Blue...both lines are blue."

Conrad's eyes grew wide with disbelief and fear. "I..." he said and then took the result dish from Amanda. The first thing his scared eyes witnessed were two blue lines. "The lines are both…blue…"

Sarah felt more tears of joy explode from her eyes. "Oh, Conrad!" she cried, running to her husband and wrapping her arms around him. "We're pregnant…we're going to have a baby!"

Conrad felt tears begin to drip from his shocked eyes. He dropped the result dish onto the wooden floor and hugged Sarah as tightly—and gently—as possible. "A baby…Sarah… we're pregnant…but how?"

"God," Sarah cried in a joyful voice. "A miracle…"

"A miracle?" Conrad whispered and then yelled: "A miracle! Sarah…we're going to have a baby…a real baby…you and me…mommy and daddy…diaper changes…three o'clock feedings…spit-up all over my clothes…baby bottles…baby clothes…no sleep…"

"I know…isn't it great!" Sarah laughed as her mind rejoiced and temporarily forgot that a monster was slowly slithering toward Snow Falls. "A baby…we're going to be a mommy and a daddy." Sarah reached out her arms and pulled Amanda to her. "June Bug, you're going to be an aunt…"

Amanda felt tears of her own begin to fall. "Oh, I'm so happy for you…Praise God…oh, our prayers have been answered!"

Sarah didn't know if she wanted to start dancing, or faint, or simply stand very still. Her emotions were raging in every direction possible—emotions of absolute joy and shock rather than fear and sadness. "Oh…a mommy…I'm going to be a mommy." Sarah touched Conrad's face with a loving hand. "You're going to be a daddy."

Conrad gently leaned forward and kissed his wife. "You,

me, and the baby makes three." Mittens, who was lying close to Andrew's office door, let out a bark. Conrad laughed. "Okay, girl…you're included."

"And what about me, you silly bloke?" Amanda demanded.

"You're forever," Sarah promised and kissed Amanda's cheek. "Oh, this…I would have never imagined…my goodness."

Amanda's face glowed with happiness. "David was only a little shepherd boy and Goliath was a giant, love."

Amanda's words suddenly forced Conrad's mind to turn around and focus on the Lara Wilston, who was daring the storm in order to deceive her prey. "Lara Wilston," he whispered, feeling his chest tighten with fear.

"What, honey?" Sarah asked.

Conrad grabbed Sarah's hand and rushed her back to his office. "Lara Wilston. Sarah, that monster is still out in the storm," he explained and then called Pete. Pete picked up on the second ring. "Anything new, Pete?"

"Jim left my office about half an hour ago. Give him time, Conrad," Pete fussed. "I was getting ready to go get a bite to eat. I should be—"

"Sarah's pregnant, Pete," Conrad blurted as Amanda entered the office. "We don't have time to tap dance on this case."

"Pregnant?" Pete repeated as if Conrad had punched him in the face. "Conrad, are you putting moonshine in the water?"

Conrad held out the phone to Sarah. "You talk to him."

Sarah smiled, took the phone with a nervous hand, and

said: "Pete, this is Sarah. I…just found out the good news. I'm pregnant."

"What?" Pete gasped. He sprang to his feet, spit out a half-smoked cigar, and nearly spilled a cup of coffee all over his desk. "Kiddo, don't mess with me, okay? I…you better…" Pete heard his voice begin to shake.

"I'm pregnant, Pete," Sarah promised as fresh tears began to fall from her sweet eyes. "God intervened on my behalf."

Pete stood in shock. If Sarah was pregnant, that meant… that meant the rules of the game had just dramatically changed. A new, innocent, and precious life was now at risk. "Sarah, I…I need to get on the phone with Jim and put a fire under him."

"Leave Jim alone, you old fuss," Sarah laughed at Pete. "You know as well as I do Jim is working against the clock, too and—" Suddenly Sarah stopped laughing as her mind began to hear the laughing of a deranged snowman who was standing somewhere deep in the shadows of her fear. "The snowman… Lara Wilston," Sarah whispered as her left hand, out of a motherly instinct, reached down and touched her tummy.

"Lara Wilston is moving toward your location," Pete pointed out in a worried voice. "The only thing we have going for us is that Lara Wilston doesn't know we know who she really is…doesn't know Jim has a friend monitoring her financial transactions." Pete began searching for his cigar, found it, and shoved it into his mouth. "We have time to set a trap, kiddo. But we're going to have to be very smart because Lara Wilston isn't stupid…and neither was the Back Alley Killer."

"Yes, I know," Sarah assured Pete as the snowman continued to laugh at her. *You're never going to be a mommy,*

Sarah…Lara's going to win…you're going to be swallowed by the darkness…forever! "The Back Alley Killer was extremely clever."

"Which means we're going to have to be smarter," Pete demanded. "Kiddo, you're going to have to use every ounce of brains you have, do you hear me? You're going to have to… walk back into all those rainy alleys and face the monster all over again."

Fear grabbed Sarah's heart and began squeezing so hard that, for a moment, she believed her heart was going to explode. "Pete—"

"Listen to me!" Pete barked, hating to raise his voice to a pregnant woman. "You have an innocent life living inside of you now! You're not just out there protecting your own back side, kiddo, understand? So you better kick the dust off those brains of yours and get back into the back alleys…and get into the mind of Natalie Jones…or Lara Wilston…whatever you want to call her. In my book I call her a killer."

Sarah closed her eyes, saw the hideous snowman step out of a dark shadow, hiss at her, and then fade away. "Okay, Pete…I understand what I have to do," she said and began rubbing her tummy. "I have to go back to being Detective Sarah Garland for a while…and I will."

"That's my girl." Pete clapped his left hand down onto his desk. "That's the tone I miss hearing in your voice."

"Understand the killer…that's the first thing you taught me, Pete," Sarah continued, keeping her eyes closed, searching the dark shadow the snowman had vanished back into. "Okay, you monster…I created you…and now I'm going to destroy you," she whispered and, within the deepest part of her mind that was forbidden to the world, Sarah charged into the dark shadow and vanished. "Okay, Pete," she whispered, watching the woman in her mind step through the dark shadow and enter a rainy alley filled with dumpsters and trash cans, "I'm back in the alleys." *You'll never win!* the snowman hollered as it slithered behind a dumpster. *You'll never win, Sarah...*

Conrad watched the joy that was covering his wife's sweet face vanish. A hard, stone cop's face replaced the joy—a look only a cop could understand; a look that only a woman who understood murder could own. "Okay, then," he said and nodded, "let's get to work."

Amanda studied Sarah's face, saw with her own eyes her best friend change from a scared woman who only wanted to become a mother into a hard, stone cop, and slowly folded her arms. "This is the way it has to be for now," she whispered, looking at Conrad. "Give me my gun out of your top desk drawer. It's time to face a killer."

Conrad pulled open the top desk drawer, handed Amanda a Glock 19 that the woman had become very familiar and skilled with, and then focused on Sarah. Sarah slowly opened her eyes—only the eyes Conrad saw appear before him belonged to a woman who was still living in Los Angeles working on deadly homicide cases; Sarah Spencer had temporarily fallen into hibernation.

"Pete," Sarah spoke in a cop's voice, "stay close to Jim. In the meantime, I'm going to see how I can use this storm to my advantage."

"Got it, kiddo," Pete promised. He told Sarah bye and then called Jim.

Sarah put down the phone, walked over to the office window, and began studying the raging storm that was howling and screaming outside. "There has to be a way to use this storm to our advantage, but how?" she asked as the detective inside of her mind began exploring a wet, shadowy alley, searching for a killer as a hideous snowman watched from behind a greasy dumpster. "There has to be a way…"

Far away, Lara Wilston, battling a dangerous snow-soaked road that only a truck with four-wheel drive could operate on, studied the storm that was following the new truck she had bought. "I'm on my way, Sarah," she hissed. "You won't expect me to show up in this storm, but I will. If this truck can't make it, the snowmobile will carry me. One way or the other I will arrive in the storm…and when I do…goodnight, mommy…for life," Lara hissed again and then forced her deranged, vicious mind to focus on nothing but the snow-covered road.

What Lara didn't know was that Sarah was fully aware the monster in the storm was loose. Yes, Lara was a brilliant woman, but what her mind could never fully understand was that cops—good cops—never let one another down, not even in a raging storm.

Chapter Eleven

"Leave town?" Amanda asked in a shocked voice.

"Yes," Sarah explained. "We now know, thanks to Jim Wallace, that Lara Wilston's real name is Natalie Jones. Lara isn't aware that we are in possession of her real name. She also isn't aware that we know she's on the move." Sarah touched her tender tummy with a loving hand. "Lara is moving toward Snow Falls to play a very sick game that will end in murder. We need to intercept her goal and create a set of new rules."

Conrad rubbed his chin. "Make her chase us, right?"

"Exactly." Sarah nodded, keeping her hand over her tummy. "We educate Lara by leaving a note at the cabin as well as the coffee shop. Lara is sure to visit one of the two." Sarah lowered her eyes down to a box of donuts sitting on Conrad's desk. "I need real food," she complained. "Anyone up to making a trip down to the coffee shop?"

Amanda pointed a finger at Conrad. "On your feet, daddy," she ordered.

Conrad let out a tired but compliant smile. "So it begins,"

he said. He stood up and grabbed a pencil and pad of paper. "Okay, ladies, what's your order?"

"There's still plenty of lunch meat in the refrigerator," Sarah told Conrad. "Make us some sandwiches…with tomatoes, cheese, pickles, lettuce, and add in a little cayenne pepper that is sitting in the spice rack hanging next to my office door."

"And don't forget the bags of potato chips and cinnamon rolls," Amanda ordered as her mouth began to water. "I love my chips."

"You ladies have a regular restaurant," Conrad stated as he scribbled down the order.

"Well, we thought offering sandwiches along with the coffee might be a good idea," Amanda explained in a proud voice.

"So far the idea is really paying off," Sarah added, took Amanda's arm, and produced a supportive smile. "Our profit margin has risen almost two percent."

"Almost two percent, huh?" Conrad asked and fought back a grin. "Yeah…that's something, honey."

"Should you shoot the bloke or should I?" Amanda asked.

Conrad grinned, grabbed his coat off a wooden coat rack standing next to the front door, and looked at Sarah. "Any vacation spots in mind?"

"Los Angeles," Sarah told Conrad. "Once this storm ends, we leave town."

Conrad tossed a thumb toward the front door. "Honey, that storm outside is hanging tough. It's likely Lara might reach us before we can leave town."

"I don't think so," Sarah objected, grabbing a plain donut and munching on it. "Conrad, Lara is acting out of anger right now. Anyone with common sense knows not to travel in this type of storm. Lara is going to become tangled in numerous problems before she reaches Snow Falls. My guess is she might actually be forced to turn back."

Conrad turned to the front door of the police station and listened to the screaming, cruel winds screeching through the bars of the storm. No human could go for more than half an hour in the storm without being forced to seek shelter. A woman in a truck hauling a snowmobile—a woman traveling on icy, snow-caked roads, would surely be forced to finally hunker down in some little town that dotted the map between Anchorage and Snow Falls. Killer or no killer, Lara Wilston was not invincible. Conrad simply worried that the darkness consuming the woman's heart would somehow give Lara some strange superhuman strength—a strength fueled by hatred—that would allow her to navigate the storm without any problems. "You could be right, Sarah, but I don't want to take that chance. We need to prepare for Lara's arrival just in case."

Sarah wanted to explain to Conrad the strange sense of confidence that was swelling up inside of her heart like a tidal wave. Somehow, some way, a powerful voice was assuring Sarah that Lara would not reach Snow Falls before she managed to make tracks for Los Angeles. But how could she put into words the voice that was speaking inside of her heart? "Conrad...honey, I think we're going to be able to leave town before Lara arrives," Sarah tried to assure her husband.

Amanda studied Sarah's thoughtful eyes and spotted a glow beginning to form. "I think your wife is right," she told Conrad, feeling relief wash through her worried mind. "I think this storm is turning out to be our friend rather than our enemy."

Conrad turned and looked into Sarah's eyes. He was shocked to see his wife's eyes glowing—or at least Sarah's eyes seemed to be glowing. As he looked into the glow, a sudden calm and peace took hold of his mind, at least for the time being. "Okay, honey…we'll assume Lara will arrive to find us gone. But then what? What will we do once we reach Los Angeles? We have to track Lara…catch her…somehow standing in a puddle of guilt."

"Exactly," Sarah told Conrad. "We know who Lara truly is and we're going to use that truth to trap her. But until then, if Lara calls, we have to play dumb." Sarah polished off her donut. "Jim Wallace has sent us a powerful weapon. That man is a blessing, so let's use the blessing that has been sent to us and play smart."

Conrad could plainly see that Sarah's mind was forming a plan. He decided not to press the subject any further in order to give his wife some breathing room. "I'll go get the food."

"Bring back more coffee," Amanda ordered and then pointed at Sarah. "Decaf for your wife, please, sir."

"Decaf?" Sarah asked and then touched her tender tummy. "Uh…yes, decaf." She smiled at Conrad.

Conrad smiled back, kissed Sarah, tossed the hood attached to his coat over his head, and pulled open the front door. "Give me at least an hour," he yelled over the raging winds. He placed his right arm over his face and pressed out into the storm, closing the front door behind him.

Usually the sight of Conrad fighting his way out into the storm would have worried Sarah. At that moment in time, however, she simply felt at ease—as if Conrad was simply riding down the street to buy a gallon of milk. The strange sense of peace that was suddenly controlling her mind felt like a warm blanket that had just left the womb of a hot dryer. "Donut?" she asked Amanda.

"Sure, why not add on a few tons, love?" Amanda joked, grabbing a chocolate donut and scarfing it down. "So," she said, "what now?"

"Pete," Sarah pointed out, taking Amanda's hand and walking her best friend back to Conrad's office. "June Bug," she explained, sitting down behind Conrad's desk, "when I worked the crime scenes of Los Angeles there was a certain neighborhood that I always tried to steer clear of."

Amanda sat down in a chair facing Sarah. "I'm all ears, love."

Sarah touched her tummy and then continued. "The neighborhood was the first…murder for me."

Amanda watched Sarah close her eyes. "Bad?"

A door in Sarah's mind opened—a cold, steel door covered with yellow police tape. Sarah watched the door open with patient eyes. As the door opened, a heavy stench of murder crept out like poisoned breath being exhaled from a monster lurking deep inside the fear of mankind.

"Yes, June Bug, it was bad," Sarah told Amanda as she walked through the door and entered a dark, rainy neighborhood lined with expensive two-story mini-mansions that belonged to the so-called privileged. "It was many years ago…and I was green," she continued as her eyes spotted a home built of lovely stone sitting in the middle of the rainy street; a dozen cop cars with their bubbles flashing were parked in front of the home. Sarah approached the cop cars as a heavy rain poured down from a marble black night sky. "A twenty-nine-year-old writer was murdered in his home by a killer who called himself 'The Spider.'"

"Creepy."

Sarah eased past the wet cops standing around all the cop cars. The cops, all dressed in police rain ponchos, were complaining and griping about the rain instead of showing compassion and worry toward the family of the murdered victim. "I could be at the bowling alley right now," one cop, a tall, young, arrogant twenty-five-year-old fussed. "The bowling tournament is next week. I don't need to be held up like this." Sarah shook her head at the cop, remembering the guy with disgust. "I had a date with Jenny," another cop complained. "It took me over a month to convince Jenny to go see a movie with me…and now look…standing out in the rain like a dummy." Sarah shook her head again and began making her way through a gate made of gray iron bars. "The 'Spider' was a thirty-one-year-old director who targeted everyone who he deemed 'offensive.'"

"Offensive?" Amanda asked. "Love, ninety percent of the people in the world today are offensive to me in one fashion or another…especially fat truckers who refuse to wear deodorant."

"The people the Spider found offensive were people who worked at the same studio that had hired him," Sarah explained as her legs began carrying the woman in her mind up a long, concrete driveway. "The Spider was upset that he was being assigned to small, cheap change movies that weren't earning him fame and fortune. He blamed the writers, the actors…everyone. In the end he decided to kill off everyone he found 'offensive' in order to further his career."

"Sounds like a real sick turkey."

"Jamison Engels was a vicious killer," Sarah promised as she reached the end of the driveway and walked through a wooden front door that had a bear carved into it. Sarah walked into an enormous living room made of delicate imported wood that had once lived in the forests of Belgium. The living room was beautiful, polished, and decorated with artwork from the late 1700s. Sarah walked her eyes around the living room and then approached Pete. Pete was smoking a cigar, standing over a dead body. "Who do we have?"

Pete tossed a weary eye at Sarah, a green-horn detective, and then shook his head. Why did he get stuck with all the rookies? Sure, he thought, Sarah was going to turn out to be a dud. "Twenty-nine-year-old writer…the Spider got to him…put knife in his back."

"A knife?" Amanda asked as a gust of powerful wind nearly shattered the office window. "Easy now," Amanda told her nerves.

Sarah kept her eyes closed. "A knife…a bullet…rope…murder is murder," she said in a deep voice. "The Spider didn't kill in any special way…just murder. The only clue we had that led us to believe each killing was carried out by the Spider was finding a dead spider on the victim's body." Inside of Sarah's mind she saw herself look at Pete. "I'll take—" Pete quickly cut Sarah off. "A dead spider was found on the body, Detective Garland. No need to search for clues. You won't find any." Sarah felt as if Pete had punched her in the heart. "There has to be some way to get this guy, Pete. This is his fourth victim." Pete looked at Sarah. "We know each victim works at the Gray Clouds Studio. We've interviewed each employee until we're blue in the face, so if you have any more suggestions, I'm all ears." Sarah sighed. Even though the dead man lying on the floor was the fourth victim of a deadly killer, he was her first homicide. "I know I'm late to the case, Pete, but I would like to find this guy." Pete rolled his eyes. "Sure, kiddo, sure," he replied in a sarcastic voice. Sarah felt anger flush in her cheeks. Pete sure was a tough guy. But what could she do? "What kind of spider was found on the body?" she asked. "A black widow, just like all the rest," Pete answered. And that's when the cop living inside of Sarah's mind fully woke up. "Maybe we should check the colleges? Speak to an arachnologist."

"Spiders…yuck," Amanda said as a cold chill ran down her spine.

Sarah saw Pete look at her with curious eyes. "A dead spider is a dead spider…black widows aren't rare in Southern California, Detective. Why would we need to talk to a spider person?" Sarah steadied her mind. "May I see the dead spider?" Pete shrugged his shoulder, yanked a plastic bag holding a dead spider in it out of his pocket, and said: "Here it is." Sarah leaned her face toward the bag and studied the dead spider. "The spider seems intact…not stepped on or even harmed." Pete shrugged again. "Yeah, so?" Sarah continued to stare at the dead spider. As she did, the spider suddenly came to life and hissed at her. "Hey!" Sarah screamed, stumbling backward and falling down. "That spider is alive." Pete looked at the dead spider. "Are you nuts? This spider is dead. Get a grip, Detective." Sarah watched Pete put the dead spider back in his pocket and then…her eyes went to the dead body. And that was when fear…the fear that took the form of a hideous snowman…began to come to life. "It has to end in that neighborhood," Sarah whispered.

"What, love?"

Sarah opened her eyes. "I have to kill the snowman," she

told Amanda. "Lara has to be the last spider that comes after me."

Amanda stared at Sarah with confused eyes. "Love?"

"I'm terrified of spiders," Sarah confessed. "Amanda…inside of my mind…all those murders I investigated…it was like being trapped in a spiderweb full of venomous spiders waiting to devour me. Even if I killed one, another spider would appear. That fear came to life on the very night I saw the black widow spider the Spider had left on his victim. It has to end…I have to kill the snowman."

Amanda struggled to make sense of Sarah's confession but knew that only her best friend understood the answer to the riddle; not all riddles made sense—not even the answers. "And you have a plan, love?" she asked.

"Not yet," Sarah confessed. "Right now, all I know is that the storm outside is actually acting like a shield that is protecting us." Sarah touched her tummy. "Lara knows I'm trying to have a baby. She killed Dr. Wester to both terrorize and taunt me while letting me know her true intentions."

"To separate you from your child."

Sarah nodded. "Another spider," she told Amanda. "Lara is special, though. She has the Back Alley Killer's venom in her. The Back Alley Killer was the deadliest spider I stepped on…" Sarah looked at the office window with deep, thoughtful eyes. "This has to be the last spider…the snowman has to die."

Chapter Twelve

Lara could no longer travel down the snow-covered road the truck she had bought was struggling to navigate. Even in four-wheel drive, the truck was struggling to travel ten feet. "This storm won't stop me," Lara growled, hitting the steering wheel. She crawled out into the snow wearing a thick, black winter coat and looked around. A remote road that bypassed all the main roads stood before her, stretching for miles, surrounded by deep, hungry wilderness that was quickly becoming soaked with darkness. Lara had located the road on a simple map, used the GPS system in the truck to help her find the road, and assumed the truck would act as a tank until she reached Snow Falls. Lara had intended to use the snowmobile to navigate Snow Falls—and in a worst-case scenario be forced to depend on the snowmobile as a secondary transportation device if the truck failed her. The worst-case scenario had arrived.

Staring up and down the road, blocking her face from the thundering, punishing, icy winds and pouring snow, Lara began to worry if she had made a fatal error by allowing her anger to take control of her mind. Sarah had insulted the Back Alley Killer…her daddy; a killer. All Lara saw inside of her mind was a smug cop grinning at her, daring her…challenging her to a battle of wits. "I killed your daddy…what are you going to do about it?" Those were the smug words that kept torturing Lara's mind. "You're going to suffer," Lara growled under her breath as her eyes searched the storm. "One way or the other I'm going to reach your little safe haven and turn your life into a nightmare. First, I'm going to kill your husband…and then your best friend…and then terrorize the town. You will suffer before I sink my fangs into you, Sarah… suffer."

Lara kicked at the snow with angry feet. Her carefully created plan and calm, clever disguise had fallen apart. "Nurse" Lara, the woman who had so cleverly played Sarah for a fool, had become an angry, distraught woman who was allowing emotion to become her enemy. Yet, Lara could not control the anger coursing through the veins running through her spiderweb. "I allowed you to feel safe, Sarah…I gave you time…now it's time to suffer," Lara hissed, speaking repetitive threats that made her feel weak and defeated.

Unable to stand the cold any longer, Lara worked her way back to the hauling trailer and began struggling to remove the gray tarp that was covering a POLARIS 600 RUSH PRO-S snowmobile—a flashy machine that the dealer promised was the absolute best; not to mention costly. The snowmobile was covered with shiny black paint with a red stripe—almost resembling a black widow spider.

"Perfect," Lara whispered as her teeth began to chatter. She yanked the tarp free, allowed the wind to take it, and focused on the snowmobile. "Fuel tank is full," she reminded herself.

"I can carry an extra gas can." Lara stopped talking as her mind suddenly began running numbers. She was still a very far distance from Snow Falls and there was no way the full tank of gas the snowmobile was holding and the gas canister sitting in the back of the truck were going to carry her across the vast distance. Lara had assumed the truck, once put into four-wheel drive, would carry her to the edge of Snow Falls, even though the dealer warned Lara that the storm pounding the northern part of the state could easily cripple any truck. Yet, the anger boiling in Lara's mind had caused her to dismiss the dealer's warning, considering the guy a male chauvinist jerk who didn't believe a woman possessed the ability to drive a truck through a storm. Now Lara was in a difficult spot.

"No," she whined, "I..." Lara threw her eyes around. There was no way the truck would be able to turn around and make it back to Anchorage. At best, Lara fretted, she would have to drive the snowmobile back thirty miles to a town she had passed and hunker down until the storm was over, then have someone dig out her truck, navigate back to a main road, and continue toward Snow Falls using a safe route. Lara was officially trapped. The storm had paralyzed her ability to navigate a deadly web.

"Okay, Sarah," she hissed, "so be it. I'll wait out the storm...but you have to do the same. When the storm ends..." Lara stopped talking as the heavy falling snow covered her shivering body. What was the point in speaking futile threats into a freezing wind? There was no point. And it was at that moment in time that Lara realized, deep down inside of her heart, that Sarah had been right: All killers were the same —connected to the same web...yet feeling as if they were unique; as if their poisonous fangs were the ones that would finally destroy mankind. The truth was, Lara realized, she was simply a forgotten, washed-out model living off the dime of an old geezer who had eyes for a pretty face; a woman who helped a killer carry out numerous murders—financed the murders, so to speak. A woman who was unmarried, unloved, and very much alone—a woman who was also…mentally insane. *Mentally insane.*

The words *mentally insane* whispered through Lara's evil mind like a snake dripping venom onto a hot, scalding desert rock. Yes, Lara admitted to the storm, she was a mentally insane human being running around disguised as a lovely face —but underneath, oh, underneath lay the face of a dark spider seeking one victim after another. Lara had never once allowed her mind to accept the truth; to accept the fact that she was mentally insane. Lara was brilliant, clever, beautiful, and dangerous—an explosive package that the world would learn to fear. Lara had planned to take the missing role of the Back Alley Killer, striking at Sarah first in order to prove to the world that she was someone to be feared—killing a famous cop would certainly strike fear into the people of Los Angeles.

But as Lara stood next to the fancy truck she had bought with money that wasn't her own, stood in a vicious storm being attacked by icy winds and sharp needles of snow, she finally admitted that…yes…she was mentally insane. Why? Why at that moment in time? Lara didn't know. Perhaps it was anger…fatigue…or even doubt…doubt that she could truly take over the role of the Back Alley Killer. Oh, how Lara wanted to punish the world; how she hated the world, hated mankind…hated being alive. Oh, how Lara wanted to make others suffer in order to feel alive; perhaps, she thought, that's why her daddy turned into a killer? But the truth was, Lara realized, as her eyes looked up and down the stormy road, there was no excuse for murder. The Back Alley Killer killed because he was a killer—a mentally insane, deranged, vicious killer that was less than human…and Lara was no different. Inside she was a rotted bag of trash filled with dead waste.

These thoughts caused rage to burst through Lara's eyes and pour out like lava. "Do you think you're any different, Sarah?" she asked. "You spent many good years walking the shadows of different killers…what does that make you?" Unable to stand her own thoughts any longer, Lara focused on the snowmobile. It was time to get moving. But as Lara began the tedious task of unloading the snowmobile, a strange sound appeared. Startled, Lara threw her head up as the gate connected to the hauling trailer dropped down into the snow. And there, standing no more than four yards from her, a hideous snowman appeared wearing a black leather jacket and chewing a candy cane. "If you want to understand," the snowman hissed at Lara, "read the books."

Lara stared at the snowman in shock. Was she truly seeing a hideous snowman chewing a candy cane? "What…are you?" she asked in a frightened voice.

The snowman narrowed its eyes and began slithering through the snow. "Go back to the town you passed, Lara, and begin reading every book Sarah wrote. You will find out her secret and understand how to defeat her," the snowman growled. "Go back to the town you passed and start reading… every book…every single word Sarah wrote. Do you understand?"

Lara stared into a set of red, pulsating eyes. Clearly, she thought, she had finally arrived at a place inside of her mind that was completely void of reality. "Who are you?"

"I'm the Snowman killer." The snowman grinned.

"I...read about you," Lara stammered. "You were in Sarah's books."

"You read about me," the snowman snapped at Lara, "but you didn't understand me!" The snowman finished off his candy cane and then reached out an icy claw toward Lara's face. "You didn't understand me, Lara. You focused on the killers...but you didn't focus on me."

Lara saw the snowman reach out his icy claw. She stumbled backward and fell down onto the snow. "Stay back!" she hollered. "You're not real!"

The snowman grinned. "I'm real to you," it warned Lara. "I'm real because somewhere deep inside of you, Lara, you have realized that I hold the secret to Sarah...I wouldn't be standing here if you didn't."

Lara stared up at the hideous snowman with eyes that slowly adopted curiosity over fear. "What are you talking about?" she demanded. "I've read every book Sarah wrote... dribble...nonsense...useless stories that entertain the minds of idiots."

"Is that so?" the snowman asked in a clever voice. He withdrew his icy claw, pulled out a second candy cane from the pocket of the leather jacket he was wearing, and grinned. "Sarah is a very brilliant woman, Lara. She adds hidden... secrets into her stories...secrets that reveal who she truly is. That's why Sarah used a penname instead of her real name... she's scared, Lara...scared."

Surely, Lara thought, she was going completely insane. The snowman was...was...a figure her demented imagination was creating. Yet, as she stared at the snowman, a voice inside of her mind—a small voice that still clung to a very thin strand of intelligence—ordered her to listen. If the snowman was present, that meant Lara's mind was attempting to reveal a hidden treasure she had somehow neglected to locate. "I'll go read the books," she promised.

"Good." The snowman grinned as it chewed on the candy cane. "And as you read each book, Lara, pay careful attention to the snowman…the snowman is the secret."

Lara carefully crawled to her legs. Her plan to destroy Sarah had begun with intelligence, brilliance, and control. Lara had contacted Sarah, pretended to be a nurse, and had deceived her victim. Lara's next step was to allow Sarah time to realize that "Nurse Lara" was a fake in order to begin taunting her victim. But one simple phone call made in a coffee house filled with minds consumed with trash had altered Lara's clever plan of attack and transformed her into a mentally insane woman talking to a snowman on a remote Alaska road crippled by a dangerous storm. Lara was undergoing a transformation, slowly shedding her human beauty and finally allowing the evil of her mind to dress her face.

"I'll read the books," she promised the snowman again, ignoring the icy winds and heavy falling snow and feeling as if she were falling into a hypnotic state. "I'll read the books… and I'll find Sarah's secret…and make her suffer. She killed the Back Alley Killer. She killed the only man who ever cared for me…now she will suffer."

"Good." The snowman grinned again. "Read the books, Lara…slowly…carefully. This storm is very powerful. This storm will last for another two days. You watched the weather report. Use your time wisely."

"I will," Lara assured the snowman. She turned her eyes to the snowmobile and grinned. "I will use my time wisely as I'm sure Sarah is taking the same route. Yes, right now Sarah is creating a trap for me. I have to stay one step ahead of her…" Lara stopped talking, threw her eyes at the snowman, and grinned again. "Perhaps trying to reach Sarah is the wrong approach. Perhaps I need to make Sarah come to me?" she asked the snowman as the image of Pete entered her mind. "Yes, of course," Lara said, feeling a dark, evil patience suddenly destroy the anger that was forcing her to race toward Snow Falls. "Perhaps it's time I changed course and went after a smaller fly?"

The snowman sneered. "Read the books very carefully," it told Lara and then started to melt down into the snow. "The secret to Sarah is in her books…in the snow…focus on the snowman…the snowman…"

Lara watched the snowman melt down into the snow and then, without any regard to the storm—as if she had turned into a robot that had been reprogrammed—she worked to free the snowmobile from the hauling trailer, retrieved a black suitcase from the cab of the truck, and then started back down the remote road with murder flashing in her eyes.

Far away in Snow Falls, Sarah watched night fall as she ate a turkey sandwich. "Call Pete for me, honey," she told Conrad as her eyes stared out at the storm.

Conrad picked up the phone on his desk and called Pete. Pete picked up on the first ring. "Sarah wants to speak to you."

"Put her on."

"Here you go." Conrad held the phone out to Sarah.

Sarah turned away from the office window, walked to Conrad's desk, and took the phone with her left hand, keeping the sandwich her tummy was hungering for secured in her right hand. "Pete, 897 Palm Wave Street."

Pete, who was sitting at his desk smoking a cigar and going through the folder Jim had brought him, froze. "Are you sure, kiddo?" he finally asked. "You swore—"

"I have to, Pete," Sarah whispered in a shaky voice. "I'm going to lure Lara to 897 Palm Wave Street…and end it, Pete. I'm going to kill the snowman in the same house…I was almost killed in."

Conrad looked up at Sarah with confused eyes. "Killed?" he asked. "Sarah, you never told me—"

"Pete, whoever is living in that house…get them out," Sarah ordered. "I'll call you tomorrow with the rest." Sarah put down the phone and looked down at her husband. "Honey," she said and drew in a deep breath, "years ago the first killer I went after nearly killed me. The fear…has never left me. Before our innocent child is born…the snowman has to die. It has to end…the fear has to be destroyed in the same place it was born."

Conrad didn't know what to say so he said nothing.

Outside, the storm raged on—inside of Sarah's heart, a different storm raged on.

Chapter Thirteen

The storm ended. Snow Falls began to dig out and clean up. Sarah, Conrad, and Amanda were packing a suitcase apiece instead. "Andrew reported that plows are clearing the main roads," Conrad called out to Sarah from a warm kitchen. "We should be able to reach Timber Trails in about an hour and catch the bush plane and fly to the Anchorage airport."

Sarah had no desire to cram herself into a small bush plane with her husband and best friend, but it was urgent she reach the Anchorage airport as soon as possible. "Amanda is at home packing. We have to swing by her cabin and pick her up in an hour," she called back, studying a brown suitcase sitting on the kitchen table. Mittens was asleep on her doggy bed. "Mrs. Apworth will be by to check on you, honey. I just hope she doesn't complain about this green dress I'm wearing. Mrs. Apworth always insists I wear blue." Mittens wagged her tail. She loved Mrs. Apworth—the old lady was a bit crazy but very loving and fun to be around. "I—" Sarah began to speak again but stopped when the kitchen phone rang. A cold chill ran down her back. "Lara," she whispered. She called out for Conrad and answered the call. "Hello?"

"I'm close to Snow Falls, Sarah," Lara lied. "It was quite a storm, wasn't it? But not enough to keep me away."

Sarah waited until Conrad ran into the kitchen before speaking. It was time to bring Sarah Garland back into the picture. "Our roads are still impassable, Lara, so knock off the lies," she snapped, deliberately playing stupid. "You're still in Anchorage." The truth was, Sarah knew Lara had holed up in a small town outside of Anchorage called Deep River and, according to Jim, had then gone back to Anchorage and purchased a flight to Los Angeles. Pete had been notified. "I've been living in Alaska long enough to understand the weather and the roads, Lara. Snow Falls is too far north and only one road leads into town…that road is impassable at the moment."

Lara grinned as she lounged outside the Anchorage airport in her truck. "Think what you will, Sarah," she teased, speaking in a new voice that Sarah found alarming. "I have decided to break all the rules and conduct a full frontal assault…at the time of my choosing, of course."

Sarah played smart. "I'm not afraid of you, Lara," she stated in a firm tone. "I've dealt with your kind all my life. You know where I live. I'm not running."

Lara grinned again. Sarah was falling right into her trap. Perfect. "You can run, Sarah, but I'll find you."

"I'm not running from you, Lara…and I know that's not your real name." Sarah looked at Conrad with intelligent eyes. She needed to give Lara space before dropping the bomb. "I have every cop in Anchorage searching for you. You won't get far."

"Is that so?" Lara asked Sarah, feeling in full, absolute

control. She had reread every book Sarah had written. The snowman…oh yes, the snowman. "Tell me, Sarah, do you like snowmen?"

Sarah froze. "Snowmen?" *Snowmen…snowmen!* A hideous voice laughed at Sarah. *Oh, let it snow let it snow let it snow, Sarah…let it snow!* Sarah closed her eyes and saw the hideous snowman appear wearing a black leather jacket and chewing a candy cane. *She knows, Sarah…Lara knows!*

"Sarah?" Conrad whispered. "Sarah…are you okay?"

"I'm okay," Sarah whispered back, opening her eyes and focusing on the phone call. "I stopped being scared of the boogeyman years ago, Lara."

"Is that so?" Lara asked, glancing down at the very first book Sarah had written, and smiled. "Well, we'll see, Sarah, we'll see. In the meantime, watch your back because I'm very close to you…closer than you realize," she lied.

"Stop lying," Sarah ordered Lara in a tough cop voice even though she felt shaken. "Lara, I know you're in Anchorage." Sarah looked at Conrad. Conrad folded his arms over his black sweater and waited. It was time to drop a bomb on Lara before Lara slithered away. "Or should I say…stop lying, Natalie Jones!"

It was time for Lara to freeze up. "What…did you say?" she asked Sarah in a dumbfounded voice. Had Sarah actually called Lara by her real name? If so…how? Anger flared up in the woman's cheeks. "What did you say?" she asked, as if her voice had turned into poison.

"Natalie Jones," Sarah snapped. "I know who you are, Lara. I know your real name. What? Did you think I wouldn't find out? Lara, give me a break. I'm a cop…and I always discover the truth. I know you're the daughter of that—"

Sarah paused. It was really time to shake Lara up. "I know you're the daughter of that loser people called the Back Alley Killer. That guy was a ten-cent loser that I took down with a feather." Sarah's goal was to infuriate Lara enough to actually make the woman change course and focus her attention directly on Snow Falls. "You want revenge because I put poor daddy dearest six feet under."

"Shut your mouth, you stupid cop!" Lara exploded as her mind dropped into a room filled with rage rather than remaining in a calm, dark room filled with control and power. "I'm going to kill you!"

"Come and get me, Lara…or should I say…come and get me, Natalie Jones," Sarah deliberately taunted Lara. "It was very clever of you to marry a rich old man and use his money to create a new identity, wasn't it? Sure, it was." Sarah drew in a calm breath. "Money can have certain benefits…and downfalls, Lara. For instance, I just so happen to know you turned back from Deep River and returned to Anchorage, where you bought a plane ticket to Los Angeles."

Lara's eyes began to drip with red, poisonous fury. "You're a dead woman!" she yelled in a futile tone.

Sarah looked at Conrad, who was allowing her to drive the car without offering any backseat advice. "The rules of the game have changed, Lara," she explained. "I'm going to make a new set of rules that you're going to follow. Is that clear?"

"What do you want?" Lara hissed.

"You and me…Snow Falls…one final showdown," Sarah told Lara. "I'm a retired cop. While I want the authorities to snatch you up, they really don't have any justification to charge you for Dr. Wester's murder. I know you'll make bail and vanish into the wind. After all, a woman who has over twenty million dollars isn't stupid, is she?"

Lara nearly ground her teeth into powder. "You have violated my personal rights," she snapped, sounding foolish. "I'm…" Lara didn't know words of destruction to throw at Sarah. She was sounding weak and childish. "All right, Sarah…a showdown. But how do I know you're not setting a trap?"

Sarah touched her tummy. "Lara, you know I'm trying to have a baby. The last thing in the world I will tolerate is for you to remain alive…haunting me…causing me to jump at every shadow…worrying about my child's safety for the rest of my life. No…it's either you or me…prison is a no-go for the likes of you."

Lara sat silent for a minute. Was Sarah speaking the truth? She didn't know. "All right," she finally spoke, deciding to once again alter her plans and return to Snow Falls. Sarah had to die. Lara had hoped to kill Sarah in the same alley she had first encountered the Back Alley Killer…but now it seemed Sarah would have to die the hard way. Still, Lara thought, feeling disappointment overcome her anger, she still had the snowman. Victory was certainly waiting in the distance. "Name the rules."

"Snow Falls…you have five days to get here. If you don't show up, I'll turn over your information to the FBI and have some of my old cop friends place some heavy drugs in your fancy canyon home in California." Sarah despised sounding like a bad cop, but what choice did she have? Lara had to be controlled. "Are we on the same page?"

Lara watched thick, wet snowflakes land on the windshield of her truck. "You're trying to twist my arm," she growled at

Sarah. "I don't like being threatened." The idea of having a couple of bad cops plant drugs in her home made Lara want to rip the steering wheel out of the truck.

"I know where you live, Lara. I know your bank account number. I know where your personal car is parked in Los Angeles. I know what restaurant you visit on a regular basis…money leaves a nice trail." Sarah looked at Conrad again. She was forcing Lara to turn to cold, hard cash—and that's exactly what Sarah wanted, for the time being. "Every time you use your bank card I know."

Lara closed her eyes. All she had was her bank card and some cash. It had never once occurred to her mind to create different financial accounts to depend on just in case her true identity became exposed. Now she was backed into a corner, forced to play by the rules of a smug cop. "No," she hissed, picking up Sarah's book and studying the creepy snowman staining the front cover. "I had it all figured out…I had you all figured out…the game is not lost…you're a dead woman." Lara let out a venomous breath. "Sarah, you are going to die," she promised.

"We'll see," Sarah fired back. "You have five days, Lara…or else. In the meantime, I want you to use your bank card only once a day. Each transaction better show me you're moving toward Snow Falls, is that clear?" Sarah looked down at her hands and steadied her mind. "Draw out enough cash to help you get to Snow Falls, no more, no less. Food…gas… lodging…nothing else. Make each transaction at a gas station."

Feeling trapped, Lara knew she had two options: obey or run. However, Lara feared if she ran, Sarah would honor her word and have some of her old friends plant drugs in her home. Sure, she could leave the country, but surely, she worried, a warrant for her arrest would be created. How would she ever be able to reenter the country without being arrested unless she sneaked back in illegally? By then, tracking Sarah down to kill the woman would become more of a chore than a sweet dessert. No, Sarah had to die…in Alaska…as soon as possible. "The snowman," Lara whispered. "Use the snowman."

"Are you listening to me, Lara?" Sarah asked.

"The snowman is listening," Lara fired at Sarah. "You know all about the snowman, don't you, Sarah?"

Why was Lara mentioning the snowman? Sarah wasn't sure. However, each time the killer mentioned the snowman, a shiver of fear dripped into her heart. "I know the snowman, Lara," she confessed.

"Oh, yes you do," Lara confirmed in an evil, soulless tone. "The snowman is coming for you, Sarah. I'm coming for you." Lara studied the snowman staring at her from Sarah's book. "I'll play by your rules…you can threaten me all you want, but once I arrive, we're going to play by my rules."

"We'll see," Sarah replied, feeling very cold and suddenly uncertain of the plan she had worked so carefully to create. *It's the fear, Sarah…the fear,* the snowman laughed. *You're scared… you've always been scared.* Sarah closed her eyes, saw the snowman standing out in her front yard wearing a leather jacket and chewing a candy cane, and moaned.

"Sarah?" Conrad asked.

"It's all right," Sarah whispered, staring at the snowman, "it has to be this way for…now." Sarah flung her eyes open. "You have five days, Lara," she warned. "When you arrive in Snow Falls, call my home. I'll be waiting."

"Yes, you will," Lara promised. "Until then I'll play by

your rules, Sarah…while you count down the seconds to…the last spider bite." With those words, Lara ended the call, leaving Sarah feeling even colder.

"You did good," Conrad promised, watching his wife hang up the phone.

"Lara will come to Snow Falls." Sarah nodded, wondering again why the killer mentioned the snowman. "We have five days, Conrad."

Conrad studied Sarah's eyes. "What's the matter?" he demanded.

"I…I'm not sure," Sarah confessed. She walked over to the kitchen table and closed the suitcase. "Hurry and finish packing, okay, honey? The sooner we leave for Los Angeles, the better."

Conrad leaned against the refrigerator and folded his arms. "Not until you talk to me, Sarah," he demanded. "I'm your husband, remember?"

"Lara mentioned the snowman…why…how?" Sarah told Conrad in a deeply troubled voice. "Why did that awful woman mention the snowman?"

"I don't know," Conrad answered, feeling helpless to offer his wife a warm blanket of comfort.

"The killer who first appeared in Snow Falls…that model. She built the snowman in my front yard."

"I remember," Conrad told his wife and then grew silent.

Sarah left the kitchen table and walked to the back door. "I've come close to dying many times in Snow Falls, Conrad. Once I chased a killer through the woods behind my house… the killer knocked me unconscious. If Amanda wouldn't have found me, I would have frozen to death." Sarah shook her head. "The snowman…the fear…it was either fight or let the fear destroy me…drive me insane."

Conrad unfolded his arms, walked over to Sarah, and put his hands down onto her tender shoulders. "I never knew, Sarah. You always appeared so strong…in control."

Sarah touched Conrad's loving hands. "It all began on the night I arrived at the home of the man the Spider killed. The fear was born…and then…when the Spider began stalking me…nearly killed me in the same home I saw the black widow spider…I became a victim, a victim of a deep, dark fear that would never stop haunting me."

Conrad pulled Sarah closer. "You managed to kill the Spider, Sarah…and you'll kill the snowman," he promised.

"I managed to grab my gun before I was strangled to death," Sarah corrected Conrad. "For those horrible few seconds, as the Spider was strangling me, the snowman came to life…but I didn't know it at the time. I…shot the Spider… killed him…but…the spider bite was fatal." Sarah turned and faced Conrad. "Before our child is born, the snowman has to die," she declared in a shaky voice. "We have Lara where we want her, but she's still very dangerous. We have to play smart…be smart…now please, go finish packing and let's get moving."

Conrad studied Sarah's eyes. He saw a scared woman and a determined cop fighting one another. Fortunately, the cop was winning the battle. "All I have left to pack is my toothbrush," he promised and hurried away, leaving Sarah to her thoughts and the falling snow outside.

Chapter Fourteen

A gust of warm, salty air struck a tall palm tree instead of icy winter air. The air felt wonderful compared to the freezing winds Sarah was used to—yet, Sarah thought, as she walked into the brick building holding Pete's office, the air was stained with crime, smog, hate, and violence; elements of a decaying society that would never heal. "At least we're in Los Angeles," Sarah whispered, feeling the air grab a deep gray dress that made her look very much like a cop.

Conrad and Amanda, who were sitting across the street in a white SUV, watched Sarah enter the building with careful eyes. "Well," Amanda said, munching on a candy bar and holding a cherry soda, "I guess this is the part where we wait, right?"

"Right." Conrad nodded and tossed a quick eye down at the black shirt he was wearing. A stain made from hot dog chili glared up at him. "Try to eat more carefully, okay?"

Amanda snarled her nose at Conrad, held up her candy

bar, and said: "Do you see me making a mess with my treat, you fussy bloke?"

Conrad tossed a thumb at the green and white dress Amanda had so fashionably chosen to wear. "You have chocolate on your dress."

"What?" Amanda gasped. She looked down, spotted a bit of chocolate crumbs on her dress, and began making a fuss. "Oh, chocolate stains…as if nearly dying in that awful bush plane wasn't bad enough."

"We didn't nearly die," Conrad corrected Amanda as he walked his eyes up and down a street lined with palm trees. "The pilot made a safe landing."

"You call being bounced around like a ping-pong ball a safe landing?" Amanda griped as she cleared her dress.

Conrad rolled his eyes and continued to study the street. Brick buildings that were built in the 1960s lined the street—buildings that still had character to them rather than appearing like horror screams like most modern buildings did. Vehicles of different makes drove up and down the street, tittering here and there. A UPS truck was double parked with its emergency lights glaring. Yep, big city life (the poor UPS man who had to make deliveries to Snow Falls at least never had to double park). "Check your gun, okay?"

"What for?" Amanda asked Conrad. "My gun is—"

"Check your gun, Amanda," Conrad ordered in a stern voice. "Jim Wallace may be confirming that Lara Wilston is obeying Sarah's orders, but a cop learns to look in every direction."

"Do you think that evil woman is in Los Angeles?" Amanda asked Conrad.

Conrad shrugged. "We're following a trail of financial

transactions that are being made once a day, Amanda. Lara could have hired someone to make the daily transactions. This is only day two…"

Amanda quickly gobbled down the rest of her candy bar, snatched open her purse, and checked her gun. "All good."

Conrad stuck his elbow out of the driver's side window as his eyes continued to search the street. "I don't know, Amanda," he said, "my gut is telling me that Lara is around. I think Sarah feels the same…" Conrad watched a flashy red BMW drive past, ease around the UPS truck, and move on. "I think Sarah feels the same way."

Amanda felt a cold chill touch her heart. "But—"

"Sarah appeared confident that Lara would obey her and travel to Snow Falls?" Conrad asked. Amanda nodded. "Sarah was confident," he assured Amanda. "But this morning, when Sarah woke up, she told me about a dream that had haunted her."

"What was the dream?" Amanda dared to ask.

Conrad, even though the air was warm, reached out with his right hand and picked up a cup of coffee. "A snowman leaning against a palm tree…grinning." Conrad took a sip of coffee. "Sarah told me all that I needed to know."

"Well, the plan was a bit risky," Amanda admitted. "I trust Sarah with my life, but we are dealing with a killer."

"Sometimes you take a wild shot at the net when the ice is clear," Conrad told Amanda. "Sarah created a plan that she hoped would force Lara Wilston into a corner…giving us enough time to get into position."

"Oh, it's all too much," Amanda sighed. "How can a cop deal with all this…insanity? Poor Sarah, trying to outwit a killer…a deranged, ugly killer. Her mind must feel like a tossed salad right about now. Poor dear."

"Don't count Sarah out," Conrad warned. "I know my wife. Sarah always has a backup plan. Even if Lara skipped out on her part of the deal and managed to sneak back to Los Angeles, Sarah knows how to look at the back door and the front door at the same time."

Amanda sighed. How could one person…a person made of flesh and blood…create so much terror…fear…and chaos in a society that was supposedly civilized? And tracking down that person—that monster—was like trying to find a needle in a haystack. So what does a sane, rational person do? That person sets a trap, hoping the trap will catch the killer. Only a wild animal isn't going to just walk into a trap…no way. A wild, deranged animal will sniff at every log, every tree, every leaf, every piece of dirt, before taking one single step. Sure, Sarah had pushed Lara into a corner by exposing the woman's true identity, but so what? Didn't a wounded animal bite even harder? Oh, it was all too much. How in the world had Sarah survived being a homicide detective? "What if Lara is actually doing what she was told?" Amanda asked in a hopeful voice.

"Then we have until Thursday to get into position." Conrad focused his eyes on the building Sarah had entered and waited. "Keep your eyes peeled, okay?" he told Amanda and grew silent. Amanda nodded and began running her eyes in every direction as Sarah walked into Pete's office.

"Hello, Pete."

Pete looked up from his desk, saw a beautiful woman standing in his office door, and smiled. "Hello, kiddo…you look like I feel."

Sarah closed the office door and studied Pete. Her old

partner looked exactly the same: wrinkly brown suit, messy gray and brown hair, half-smoked cigar, rugged face…yep, same old Pete. "Must be all the Chinese food," she said and pointed at all the empty Chinese food boxes sitting around the messy office.

Pete tossed the cigar in his mouth down onto a tin ashtray. "Must be," he said. He stood up, walked over to Sarah, and gave her a loving hug.

"Oh, it's so good to see you," Sarah said, melting into Pete's hug. "I've missed you…I always miss you."

"Yeah, yeah…so much mushy stuff," Pete pretended to complain. He loved Sarah as if the woman was his very own daughter. "We have work to do."

Sarah reluctantly let go of Pete. "I think Lara is in Los Angeles."

"Yeah, I kind of had a feeling," Pete confessed. "Let's take a sit and talk."

Sarah followed Pete back to his desk, sat down in a brown cushioned chair, and tried to get comfortable. "I knew I was pushing a dangerous animal into a corner, Pete," she explained as Pete sat back down. "At first I was confident Lara would do as told."

"Threatening to plant drugs in someone's home will spook anyone, especially a killer who doesn't want her face dragged across every news station in California."

"I didn't want to stoop that low," Sarah explained, "but I needed to make Lara believe I was a bad cop…the type of cop she can outsmart…just in case she bailed on my plan and decided to play foul."

"Which she did," Pete pointed out.

"I believe so," Sarah said, nodding. "I'm not sure who is

making the daily transactions for her. Andrew is staked out at my cabin—"

"He was going to answer the call when Lara Wilston arrived in Snow Falls, right?"

"Right," Sarah said. "Whoever is helping Lara might show up at my cabin. Who knows? Maybe it's just some bum or some kid Lara paid off?" Sarah slowly folded her arms. "I don't believe Lara has a silent partner."

"Okay, let's assume the woman did hire a stooge," Pete said, "and let's assume she managed to travel back to Los Angeles. Now what?"

"Lara must know about our business, Pete," Sarah told Pete in a careful voice. "Lara must know you and I run a private investigation office…she did locate Dr. Wester, after all…so I'm confident Lara knows more than we're aware of. That's why I have Conrad and Amanda outside watching the building."

Pete went for his half-smoked cigar. "So now we're the ones backed into a corner, waiting for the spider to bite, is that it?"

"No," Sarah promised. "Pete, I do have a backup plan. You taught me to always have a back door to escape through, remember?"

"Yeah, I remember," Pete said, lighting his cigar. He looked at Sarah. "I'm not a strapping twenty-year-old anymore, kiddo. Sometimes it takes everything I got to get out of bed in the morning…so go easy on my mind and get to the point."

Sarah watched Pete puff on his cigar. Years and years of memories flooded into her mind. She loved Pete and she loved his cigars. "My goal is to lure Lara to 897 Palm Wave Street, Pete."

"Yeah, I know that."

"But how? That was the question." Sarah glanced down at her tummy. "I knew when the storm ended Lara would be coming for me. I had very little time to think and form a plan." Sarah lifted her eyes and focused on Pete. "I have to kill the snowman, Pete…Lara has to be the last spider."

Pete studied Sarah's eyes. "But Lara is still loose…the spider isn't dead, kiddo."

"Not yet," Sarah continued. "I assumed…well, I hoped… by exposing Lara's true identity and backing her into a corner…I could control the woman. My intention was to bring her to Los Angeles when I was in position. I knew I was taking a dangerous risk…and now it seems that Lara has decided to try and outsmart me. But that's okay because I—"

"Have a plan," Pete grumbled. "Yeah, kiddo, you told me…now tell me your plan."

Sarah tossed a regretful eye toward the office door. "I…left some bait outside, Pete," she explained. "Conrad knows the plan…Amanda…doesn't. I…it has to be this way, Pete."

Pete continued to puff on his cigar. "Yeah, I suppose it does, kiddo," he said in a worried voice and then checked his watch. "I guess Conrad will be along any minute now."

Sarah checked the watch on her left wrist, nodding. "In about three minutes. But don't worry, this morning he slipped a tracking device into the heel of Amanda's pump." Sarah felt guilt and agony grip her heart. Allowing Amanda to become bait…blind bait…was killing her. But Sarah knew Lara wouldn't dare go after Conrad…not yet. Lara was a woman and, regardless, a woman always went after the weakest pawn first. "I hope Amanda will forgive me."

"I hope Lara Wilston is in Alaska," Pete told Sarah. He

checked his watch and waited. Three minutes later, right on time, Conrad entered the office wearing a guilty expression on his face. "Hello, Conrad."

Conrad closed the office door. "I saw the same blue SUV drive by twice," he explained. "Two men were driving. I think we've located our hit team."

"Amanda's purse?" Sarah asked, resisting the urge to run outside.

"887 Palm Wave Street…I hid the address in the purse when you and Amanda were ordering food from the hot dog stand down near the beach." Conrad looked at Sarah with deeply concerned eyes. "How do you know Lara won't harm Amanda?"

"Lara will use Amanda as bait to lure me into a trap," Sarah attempted to assure Conrad—and herself. "Lara believes we're still assuming she's in Alaska right now. We have to let her believe she is in control."

"How are you going to lure her to 897 Palm Wave Street?" Conrad asked. "Sarah, the tide is rolling in and we're not any closer to catching our killer…and I have to admit that I'm getting worried."

"Cool it, Conrad," Pete barked, shooting to his feet and walking over to Sarah. "You're talking to my partner," he said in a stern tone. "If Sarah has a plan, then you better believe the plan will work." Pete looked into Sarah's eyes. "What's the plan, kiddo?"

"A party," Sarah explained. "A masquerade party at 897 Palm Wave Street…a killer party."

Conrad and Pete looked at each other with confused eyes. "A party?" Conrad asked.

Sarah nodded. "We're going to throw a masquerade party and invite Lara. The party will take place in two days."

"How do you know the woman will show up?" Pete asked in a curious voice.

"Because I'm going to be dressed as a killer," Sarah told Pete and then checked her watch. "Conrad, the camera?"

"Inside the purse."

"And the bug?" Sarah asked.

"Planted under the collar of Amanda's dress," Conrad explained. "I planted the bug when I pretended to bump into Amanda in the lobby of the hotel."

"Camera…bug…" Pete grew silent for a moment. "Oh, I see…you're going to catch your spider…but this time have her face and voice captured in order to—"

"To make her fully accept an invitation to a killer party." Sarah nodded and patted Pete's shoulder. "Always have a back door to escape through, Pete," she said and then looked at Conrad with guilty eyes. "I sure hope Amanda will forgive me."

Outside in the white SUV, Amanda quickly checked her purse, found the hidden camera, and then checked the bug under her collar. Yes, Sarah was spilling the beans in Pete's office making Conrad and Pete believe Amanda was being used as blind bait, but Amanda was fully aware of Sarah's plan. With lightning-quick hands, she tossed on two pearl earrings—each holding a hidden bug—and then slid on a pair of reading glasses that had a tiny camera hidden in the frame (compliments of a young genius Sarah knew who could hide a camera anywhere and in anything. The young genius, grateful that Sarah had helped him turn his life around instead of sending him to jail, promised to repay the favor…and Sarah, years later, had come to collect the favor. It was good to know people). "Okay, love, I'm all set…let's just hope Pete's office is bugged like you think and Lara is listening to your every word."

Seconds later, a gray BMW sped up to the white SUV. Lara Wilston stormed out of the BMW and threw a gun at Amanda. "Into the BMW! Now!" Amanda threw her hands up into the air and did as ordered, taking her purse with her. Lara smacked the purse out of Amanda's hands, ordered the woman to remove her pumps, and then shoved her into the BMW and sped away, believing she had crippled Sarah's plan. "Now it's time to play," Lara hissed, not knowing that Sarah was in full control.

Chapter Fifteen

Lara shoved Amanda through the back door of 897 Palm Wave Street. "Inside," she snapped.

Amanda stumbled into a large, shadowy kitchen that smelled of dust, time, and fear. "Hey, easy with the glasses. I can't see a thing without them!"

Lara stepped into the kitchen and closed the back door. "Your friend thought she was very clever, didn't she?" she asked in a poisonous voice. "I have to admit, I was going to play along with her plan…well, Natalie Jones was going to play along. But then I decided to take a daring chance. After all, what did I have to lose? Nothing. But I had everything to gain."

Amanda turned and looked through the shadowy kitchen at a vicious woman wearing the blackest dress she had ever seen. "If you're in Los Angeles…who is in Alaska?"

"A couple of teenage boys who needed some extra cash." Lara grinned. "It's amazing what a couple of kids will do for a couple hundred dollars." Lara pointed a deadly gun at Amanda. "Go sit down at that table."

Amanda spotted a round kitchen table shoved into a dark corner. She let out a worried breath, walked over to the table, and sat down on a dust-soaked wooden chair. "How did you get back to Los Angeles without Sarah knowing?"

Lara opened a wooden kitchen cabinet. "It wasn't easy. My cash flow was weak, but I managed to make my way back to the Anchorage airport and find a man who didn't mind staying over a day or two. I used his boarding pass, which made my escape invisible." Lara reached into the cabinet and pulled out some rope. "Once I arrived in Los Angeles, I went to work. You see," she said, walking over to Amanda with her gun at the ready, "I have plenty of cash stored in my home. I hired a man to plant a bug in the office of that miserable old cop...and then...waited." Lara sneered. "Soon or later I knew Sarah would show up."

"Very clever." Amanda rolled her eyes.

"Shut up," Lara snapped. "Put your arms and legs behind the chair." Amanda looked up into Lara's face, saw a hideous killer, and did as told. Lara moved behind the chair and began tying Amanda's hands and legs together. Unfortunately, Lara wasn't aware that Amanda had been tied up before and had become a pro at escaping flimsily tied knots. "Your friend is going to throw a party in two days. I'll be ready for her."

"Yeah, I bet you will," Amanda replied, pretending to sound nervous.

Lara finished tying Amanda up and then positioned herself directly in front of the woman. "Why is Sarah throwing a masquerade party?" she demanded. "What is her plan?"

"Oh, go jump off a cliff," Amanda told Lara.

Lara narrowed her eyes and shoved her gun into Amanda's face. "Talk."

"Oh…yeah…talk," Amanda whimpered. "I…Sarah is going to show up dressed up as the Back Alley Killer. All the guests are." Amanda stopped talking. Oh, she thought, Sarah's plan to push Lara into a psychological tailspin better work.

"What?" Lara asked, feeling her voice become filled with rage and confusion.

"Hey, you asked."

Lara removed the gun from Amanda's face, unaware that Sarah was moving toward her location as she spoke. "But…I was planning to use the snowman against her," she told Amanda. "The snowman came to me…I read her books…I know her fear. I know how to defeat her!" Lara yelled and kicked the kitchen table.

"Look, you asked. I told you." Amanda winced. "Don't shoot the messenger."

Lara glared down at Amanda. "I should kill you," she threatened the tied-up woman, "but I need you alive…for the time being." Lara studied the shadowy kitchen. "I'm going to destroy Sarah before she can have her little…party," she promised. "The snowman is going to devour her."

"The snowman?" Amanda asked.

"The snowman," Lara hissed. She narrowed her eyes and studied a wooden door leading into an empty pantry. A creepy snowman costume was standing inside the pantry. "Sarah fears the snowman," she told Amanda in a diseased voice. "Sarah fears the snowman. I'm going to become the Snowman killer, and Sarah is going to be my first victim."

Amanda felt a chill run down her spine. "I—"

"Shut up," Lara hissed, walking over to the pantry door and tapping her fingernails against the wood. "I hired two men to watch Sarah. I have time." Lara didn't know that Sarah had sent Conrad out as a decoy while she escaped through the back door of the office building with Pete. The two men Lara hired—the two men Conrad had seen drive past the office building in the blue SUV—were unaware that Sarah had given them the slip. They were watching Conrad sitting in the white SUV pretending to talk on a cell phone, assuming Sarah was still inside the office building. The two men, who were once both cops, had been sent to prison for turning bad. They came highly recommended by a crooked attorney Lara had contacted once she arrived back in Los Angeles. Unfortunately, the two rats were no match for Sarah. "I'm in control, now…I will create the rules."

Amanda glanced around the shadowy kitchen. The room was sure creepy, filled with the aroma of…murder. "What are you going to do?" she asked, hoping Lara was like any other killer who took pride in bragging about their murderous plan. "Please, don't hurt Sarah."

"Hurt?" Lara let out an insane laugh. "I'm going to punish Sarah…cripple her mind…and then sink my fangs into her." Lara turned away from the pantry door. "I'm going to call Sarah tonight," she told Amanda, "and order her to come to this place…this house…where the fear that controls her heart was born." Lara walked over to the back door and checked the lock. "Yes, it all began in this house. In this house the snowman was born…and in this house the Snowman killer will be born this very night," she promised Amanda in a voice that held no soul. "Sarah wanted to end her battle in this house…wanted to kill the snowman in the same house where he came alive. What Sarah doesn't know is that she's going to see the real snowman…the snowman she truly fears…come to life right before her very eyes. And then I'm going to kill her!"

"You're…insane," Amanda told Lara, feeling fury fill her eyes. "Sarah is pregnant!"

"I know." Lara grinned in such an evil way that Amanda had to close her eyes. "Not only is Sarah going to see the real Snowman killer come to life tonight, but she's going to get to see Natalie Jones carry out her vengeance. Tonight, Natalie Jones and the Snowman killer will both have victory." Lara turned away from the back door. "Isn't vengeance delicious?"

"Sarah will get you," Amanda promised.

"Will she?" Lara asked and let out a sick laugh. "Before Sarah can carry out her little insulting party, she will die." Lara pointed at the back door. "There are three ways into this house. The back door, the front door, and a door leading out to a patio. All three doors are connected to a wire that will send out a silent alarm if opened."

Amanda watched Lara walk back to the kitchen counter, pick up a little black box, and press a red button. "What did you do?"

"I activated the silent alarm." Lara chuckled. "Now the only way in and out of this house is through an old tunnel located in the basement that was used to smuggle booze into this place during the dry years. The tunnel leads right out to the greenhouse in the backyard." Lara shoved the little black box into the front pocket of her dress. "After I kill Sarah," she promised Amanda, "I will sink my fangs into you and then escape through the tunnel. When the police arrive…" Lara let out an evil laugh, "I will push another button—a button that will detonate tons of explosives I have planted around this house. Oh…the Snowman killer is going to hit the scene with a real bang!"

"You've been a busy bee, you sick monster," Amanda told Lara in a daring voice.

"Money talks," Lara said. "Now, watch and learn how a real genius works." Lara pulled a black cell phone out of her dress pocket. "Time to call Sarah's cell phone," she told Amanda. "I found Sarah's number located in her medical file. It's amazing how people expose personal information so easily, isn't it?" Amanda didn't reply. Lara grinned and called Sarah. Sarah picked up on the first ring. "Hello, Sarah."

"Where is Amanda?" Sarah demanded, deliberately playing dumb as Pete sped through the crowded streets of Los Angeles, aiming his vintage Oldsmobile toward 897 Palm Wave Street. "Leave her out of this, Lara. This fight is between me and you!"

Lara grinned again. "You thought you had me trapped in Alaska, didn't you, Sarah? Oh, yes, you thought you had won!" Lara narrowed her evil eyes. "You are so stupid, Sarah…so weak!"

"Where is my friend?"

"Shut up!" Lara yelled at Sarah. "We're playing by my rules now, Sarah. You see, I outsmarted you in Alaska…oh yes, I did. You may have discovered my true identity, but now the rules have changed. If you dare threaten me…your little British friend dies."

"What do you want, Lara?" Sarah asked as Pete swerved around a slow-moving Jaguar being driven by an old man who had made his fortune writing cheesy comedies. Pete shook his fist at the old man as he passed the Jaguar. The old man shook his fist right back.

"Come to 897 Palm Wave Street at midnight, Sarah," Lara

ordered. "Bring the old cop and your husband. We're going to have a little…party."

"I won't walk into a trap, Lara," Sarah warned, allowing her voice to sound weak.

"Come now, Sarah," Lara hissed, "you're supposed to be a homicide detective…the very woman who captured the Back Alley Killer." Lara closed her eyes, saw a hideous snowman appear before her, and grinned. "Sarah, tonight the real Snowman killer comes to life. You will have one chance to stop that from happening…one chance to save everyone you love. If you refuse to obey…oh, Sarah, the real Snowman killer will begin haunting you for the rest of your life."

Sarah closed her own eyes as a vicious fear grabbed her heart. *I'm coming to life, Sarah!* The snowman laughed as he chewed on a candy cane. *I'm coming to life…now the entire world will fear me…I'm escaping from the pages of your books…escaping! And you, Sarah,* the snowman promised through fangs dripping with venom, *will be my first victim.* "What is your game, Lara?"

"No game," Lara snapped. "You and me, Sarah. You get a knife, I get a knife, and we fight it out. The winner…wins it all."

Sarah knew Lara was lying. Lara's demented, insane mind had created a different end for Sarah—an end that Sarah feared. "Midnight…897 Palm Wave Street…but my husband and Pete—"

"Bring them or else!"

"No!" Sarah yelled, deceiving Lara. "My husband and Pete…if you win…then you're going to have to track them down. That's the rules…or…I swear I'll run."

Lara gritted her teeth. Would Sarah really desert her best

friend? Lara didn't know. But allowing Sarah to escape was not an option. "Very well. Arrive alone…no cops. If I see one cop, your friend dies and this house explodes into a fireball. Is that clear?"

"I'll arrive alone."

"When you do arrive, come around to the back door," Lara ordered. "No games, Sarah. I have eyes everywhere right now. I know you're at the cop's office. I know your husband is back outside sitting in the SUV you rented at the airport. Wherever you go…you will be watched."

"No games, Lara," Sarah promised. "You and me…one last fight…winner takes all."

Lara grinned. "Yes, Sarah…the winner takes all," she laughed and then ended the call.

Sarah put down her cell phone and looked at Pete. "Okay, partner, we're going to get one chance to get this right."

"Why didn't you tell me your plan?" Pete fussed at Sarah.

"A good cop always has a card up her sleeve, Pete," Sarah replied. "Now we have the high ground."

"Then why don't you sound so sure?" Pete asked, speeding through traffic like a wild man. Years and years ago, Los Angeles had been a good city to live in. Now the city was nothing more than an overcrowded sewer filled with crime, corruption, smog, and palm trees crying in their sleep.

Sarah turned her head and studied a line of rundown buildings holding a beauty salon, a tattoo parlor, a nail parlor, a check cashing store, a pawnshop, a comic book shop, and a DUI school. Each business appeared grimy and unfriendly. Time had certainly altered the appearance of Los Angeles, changing the landscape into a dirty sewer. Old businesses that once stood—good, decent businesses—were now nothing but fading scars attached to an oozing sore. "The city…"

"I know," Pete sighed. "I know, kiddo."

Sarah looked at Pete. "I'm sure I can capture Lara. I'm not so sure if I can kill the snowman, Pete," she confessed.

Pete glanced at Sarah, watched his partner check the hearing device attached to her right ear, and shook his head. "Kiddo, you are one of the finest cops I have ever worked with. I…what I mean to say is, even if you can't kill the fear living inside of you, well, the cop will always be present."

"I'm tired of being a cop, Pete," Sarah replied and touched her tummy. "I'm ready to be a mother. I'm ready to finally say goodbye to Los Angeles and let O'Mally's Department Store become my old friend. Last year I wouldn't have been able to tell you this because a part of me still belonged in Los Angeles, but now…it's time to say goodbye to this city, Pete…for the sake of my child."

Pete came to a red light and stopped. "Kiddo," he said in a tired voice, "I've been thinking…well," he said in a sad voice as his eyes dropped down onto his old hands, "I can never leave this city…but I can always come and see you in Alaska."

"I know, Pete." Sarah reached out and patted Pete's shoulder. "I know that you belong in Los Angeles."

"Chasing killers," Pete whispered as the red light turned green. "Okay, kiddo, let's go catch our last killer, huh?"

"Let's go, partner," Sarah said as her chest tightened. It was time to finally face the snowman…one last battle.

Chapter Sixteen

Lara, unaware that Sarah was sneaking through the greenhouse located in the backyard, checked her watch. The two men she had hired to watch Sarah were late calling in. "Idiots," she hissed, grabbing her cell phone and making a call. A rat who called himself "K" answered the call. "Report," Lara demanded.

K was nowhere near Pete's office building. Instead, he was in a rundown truck stop sitting at a back booth. "Listen," he told Lara, "we heard the voices…it sounded just like they were in the office…but then the voices stopped."

Lara felt rage flow from her eyes. "What are you talking about?" she demanded.

"We checked the office…it was a recording…she fooled us," K confessed. "Your target left a recording playing on the old man's desk. Not even the guy outside was aware your target had left the building."

"Find her!"

"Look," K told Lara, "the guy outside in the SUV showed

up in the old man's office. We tangled pretty heavy…and he put a bullet in F-Man. I barely managed to escape…man, was that guy tough. Don't expect me to risk prison time again." And with those words, K ended the call.

Lara threw down her cell phone. "Sarah," she hissed and then ran over to Amanda. "What is she up to…what is her plan?" she yelled. "Where is Sarah?"

"How should I know?" Amanda yelled back, playing dumb. "I'm sitting here all tied up…dummy."

Lara resisted the urge to slap Amanda. "Sarah knows…she has to know…she's on her way," she whispered in a frantic voice. "Oh yes, she is." Lara spun away from Amanda and vanished into the pantry. A few minutes later, she reappeared dressed in a terrifying snowman costume that nearly made Amanda scream. The snowman's face was so…hideous…so evil…so cruel…Amanda was forced to clam her eyes closed. "Say hello to the Snowman killer," Lara spoke to Amanda in a voice that didn't sound human—a voice that sounded… soulless; a deep, bottomless pit of evil.

"You're insane!" Amanda cried out. "Get away from me!"

Lara slithered through the shadowy kitchen toward Amanda holding a deadly kitchen knife in her right hand and a dead black widow spider in her left hand. "Perhaps I will kill you first," she hissed, feeling an uncontrollable desire to murder. "Perhaps I will leave you as a little welcoming present for your friend."

Amanda dared to open her eyes, looked up into the face of a snowman that held the darkest eyes she had ever seen in her life, and then focused on the kitchen knife; the blade of the knife was shadowy and hissing at her. "Get away!" Amanda screamed and, deciding there was no more time to wait, freed her hands from the rope holding her hostage. "Get away!" Without any warning, and taking Lara by surprise, Amanda threw her hands forward, shoved Lara backward, and began trying to untie her legs. Lara stumbled back into the island stove and then crashed down onto the kitchen floor. Her killer eyes slowly narrowed as she raised the kitchen knife up into the air. Amanda saw the kitchen knife and threw her hands into overtime as Lara began to rise to her feet. "Hurry… hurry…"

"Time to answer to the Snowman," Lara hissed at Amanda and began slithering toward her.

"Oh my…move…hop…move…" Amanda gasped, nearly peeing her pants, and began trying to hop toward the back door.

"There is no escape," Lara whispered as she slithered closer and closer to Amanda. "The Snowman is going to sink her fangs into you," she promised and began flashing the dead black widow spider at Amanda. "You're trapped in my web."

"You're telling me!" Amanda screamed. "Oh, Sarah… where are you?"

"Here I am!"

Lara froze. "What?" she said and slowly began to turn around.

Sarah didn't give Lara a chance to fully turn around. She aimed her gun into the air and fired off a single shot. A fierce bullet tore through the air and ripped the kitchen knife out of Lara's hand. Lara let out a vicious cry and began stumbling backward. "You go, girl!" Amanda yelled as relief began pouring through her body. Before she could say any more, Pete kicked the back door open, grabbed Amanda, and dragged her outside into the backyard, leaving Sarah alone with the snowman. "What are you doing?" Amanda demanded as bright sunlight struck her eyes.

Pete slammed the back door closed. "Sarah has to handle this alone, Amanda. All we can do is wait."

Inside the kitchen, Sarah watched as Lara backed up to the kitchen table. All Sarah saw was the deadly snowman that had been tormenting her heart. "It's time to die, Snowman."

"You fear me!" Lara hissed at Sarah. "Everything you fear…lives in me!"

Sarah walked over to the kitchen knife, kicked it across the kitchen floor, and then tossed her gun down onto the floor. "I will not be afraid anymore," she whispered, feeling terror grip her heart. Sarah was now trapped in a real-life nightmare—a nightmare that she hadn't been able to escape from in the past. She stared at the hideous snowman mask Lara was wearing as if the mask were a real snowman…a real monster. The mask was fake, but the real monster, Sarah knew, was living under the mask; her deepest fear was pulsating in the eyes of a… black widow spider dressed as a snowman. "It's you and me, Lara…one last fight."

"So be it," Lara growled.

Sarah took her foot and kicked her gun toward the kitchen knife. "Okay…now we're on even ground."

"Yes, we are." Lara grinned and, without any warning, threw her right hand down into the snowman costume and pulled out a second knife. "It's time to die, Sarah!" Lara raised the knife up into the air and charged at Sarah. *It's time to die!* the snowman living inside of Sarah's fear yelled. *I told you I would win, Sarah…you could never kill me…never!*

Sarah backed up to the island stove and dropped down into a fighting position. As soon as Lara was close enough, she threw her right leg forward and carried out a front kick. The kick caught Lara in the stomach just as she started to swing the knife she was holding at Sarah's face. Lara stumbled backward, struck the kitchen table, let out a furious cry, and charged at Sarah again. As she did, Sarah's mind walked back through time to a rainy night. *I came back to this house to have a look around…the Spider was hiding in this very kitchen. When I entered the kitchen he attacked me…and began to strangle me…his face…so monstrous…he was wearing…a snowman's mask…he started to strangle me…the mask…the snowman… staring down at me…strangling me…the snowman…the snowman. I barely managed to reach my gun…I shot the snowman…when he died…I removed the snowman mask and hid it before calling for backup…I hid the mask in my purse…to make sure the snowman could never return…but he did return…*

"Time to die!" Lara screamed.

Sarah was trapped in the past. Her eyes watched a scared woman—not a cop—shoving a hideous snowman mask into a rundown purse…and then…she saw a dead black widow spider lying next to the killer's body…only the spider wasn't dead. It was alive and crawling away…carrying the venom of the snowman away with it. Sarah wanted to kill the spider but became paralyzed…and allowed the snowman to escape.

"You…will not escape this time," she whispered, finally breaking her paralysis just as Lara swung her knife straight at Sarah's face. Sarah ducked out of the way, missing the knife by a mere inch, dived down to the kitchen floor, rolled over to her gun, and grabbed it. Lara let out a furious cry and charged at Sarah. *I came back to look around…to be brave…to face my fear,* Sarah thought as her mind continued to watch the black widow crawl away. *Instead I allowed a monster to be born…but don't worry…mommy is going to kill the monster…mommy is going to end the nightmare once and for all.* Sarah aimed her gun at Lara and fired off three solid shots—but in Sarah's mind, she fired three bullets at the black widow spider that had managed to escape.

Seconds later, a dead snowman was lying on the kitchen floor. *No!* the snowman inside of Sarah's mind cried out in agony as the snow began melting off its body and the writhing body of a black widow spider began to appear. *Yes!* Sarah yelled as she bravely approached the spider, took her hands, and began tearing it to pieces. Only each piece of the spider wasn't actually part of a real spider—each piece Sarah tore loose were pieces of hidden screams, nightmares, and fears that began to break apart in her angry hands. *Time to die!*

The last of the snow melted off the snowman, fully exposing the spider. The spider looked up at Sarah with red, furious eyes that began to dim. *I will always….be around…there are too many of us…*the spider threatened Sarah. *Maybe that's true,* Sarah replied as she finished ripping the spider apart, *but there will always be cops around, too.* Sarah backed away from the destroyed spider in her mind, walked over to the dead snowman lying on the kitchen floor, bent down, and removed the mask. The face of a woman whose real name was Natalie Jones appeared—the daughter of the Back Alley Killer.

"It's over," she whispered, replacing the mask and looking down. And there, on the floor, was a dead black widow spider. Sarah shook her head, stood up, and walked outside into the bright sunlight. "It's over," she told Pete and simply began to cry as her tender hands hugged her belly. "Mommy…won, baby." Amanda ran to Sarah, took the crying woman into her loving arms, and began to cry herself. Pete nodded, walked into the kitchen, and found the dead snowman.

Yes, the nightmare was over.

Chapter Seventeen

onrad wasn't happy that Sarah had ended up using him as a decoy rather than using Amanda as real bait. His anger passed once he walked through the back door of the warm cabin that he and Sarah called home. "I wish you would have told me, that's all."

"I wanted to, but I had to be careful, honey," Sarah replied in a tired voice. "I had one chance to catch our killer."

"That's right," Amanda said as she pushed past Conrad. "Now stop fussing and make some coffee…decaf for your pregnant wife."

Conrad dropped two suitcases down onto the kitchen floor and rolled his eyes. "Women," he complained.

Sarah smiled, kissed Conrad on his cheek, and patted her tender tummy. "You might have more women than you realize."

"Our baby is a boy," Conrad insisted and kissed Sarah back.

"We'll see." Sarah smiled again and began shaking snow off

the blue winter coat she was wearing. Amanda began to do the same. "Don't get too comfortable, June Bug."

"What do you mean, love?" Amanda asked. "It's been a long flight and—"

"And the hour is still early." Sarah beamed and pointed at the clock on the kitchen wall. "It's snowing outside…and O'Mally's is open."

Amanda froze. "Say, that's right."

"We have a lot of baby shopping to do, remember?" Sarah giggled, feeling like a new woman. All of her fears and pain were left behind in Los Angeles. The snowman was dead. Sarah was free…finally free. "I think you deserve a shopping trip, June Bug."

"We deserve a shopping trip." Amanda smiled happily and then looked at Conrad. "Okay, you bloke, cancel the coffee. Your job is to get to work on the nursery. Clear everything out of Manford's room. The little bloke can come live with me."

"Nursery…but I'm exhausted…and I have to check in with Andrew," Conrad complained. "Andrew did catch the two punks that were—"

"Oh, stop fussing and get to work," Amanda ordered Conrad. She took Sarah's hand and opened the back door. "I want kosher chili dogs, french fries, a milk shake…make that two milk shakes…and then hours and hours of shopping time…in the baby section," she giggled.

Sarah laughed. "I think I'll have some kosher chili dogs with barbeque sauce," she said and patted her tummy. "I'm starting to have these weird cravings. Last night I was craving ice cream and pickles."

"Gross," Conrad complained as he removed his leather jacket. For whatever reason, he felt that Sarah's nightmare had finally come to an end. There was a beautiful peace in the air that Conrad couldn't explain. Sure, it was cold and snowy outside—and sure the outside world was still crummy and consumed with crime—but in Snow Falls, a warm light was engulfing the town. It was as if an angel had suddenly wrapped its loving arms around Sarah and the town. "You ladies better get to O'Mally's. I'll check in with Andrew and then give Manford a call. He's due home tomorrow and we need to make sure he's going to be okay living with Amanda. I have to go pick up Mittens, too. I'm sure she's ready to come home."

"The little bloke can live with me or live in an igloo," Amanda warned and then laughed. "A frozen little bloke… that's funny."

Sarah grinned. "Behave yourself," she told Amanda. She smiled at Conrad and then walked back outside. The snow was falling in soft, gentle streams. Sarah lifted her face up into the snow and prayed a prayer of thanks. "Thank you, Lord," she whispered. She touched her tummy, smiled, and then walked with Amanda to her truck. "June Bug?"

"Yes, love?"

"I had a dream last night," Sarah explained as she began shoveling snow off the hood of her truck with her right arm.

"Oh?" Amanda asked and began helping Sarah.

Sarah nodded. "I dreamed that I was in a white tunnel… the tunnel was so beautiful and ended up in a bright field of different-colored roses." Sarah smiled. "There was a little boy and a little girl standing in the middle of the field waving at me. I waved back but I wasn't allowed to approach them…not at that moment anyway." Sarah looked at Amanda with warm, glowing eyes. "Both children promised that we would be together soon."

A gentle smile touched Amanda's face. "Love," she said, "perhaps it would be wise if we shop for twins."

Sarah looked up into the gentle snow. "Yes, June Bug, I think you're right." She giggled and then pointed toward the cabin. "Poor Conrad...how am I going to tell him we're having twins?"

Amanda giggled back. "Let's let that bloke find out for himself. In the meantime, it's off to O'Mally's, love." Amanda hugged Sarah and yelled, "We're home!"

Sarah hugged Amanda back. The nightmare was over. Now it was time to enter a good dream...a dream with no snowmen. "Okay, let's get to O'Mally's and say hello to our old friend." She laughed in absolute happiness as her hands touched her tummy. "Mommy has some shopping to do for you two."

Far away in Los Angeles, Pete received a phone call. The call left Pete shaken and wondering if he should call Sarah or not. For the time being, Pete decided to keep the call a secret.

About Wendy Meadows

Wendy Meadows, a USA Today bestselling author, delights readers with her engaging stories about women sleuths. She has penned numerous books, including the beloved Sweetfern Harbor, Sweet Peach Bakery, and Alaska Cozy series. Wendy calls New Hampshire home, where she lives with her husband, two sons, two mini pigs who have big personalities, and an adorable Labradoodle who rules the roost.

Visit her website at www.wendymeadows.com for latest releases, discounts and more!

amazon.com/author/wendymeadows

bookbub.com/profile/wendy-meadows

goodreads.com/wendymeadows